# Deep Fried Living

## Craig Hamm

This is a work of fiction. Names, characters, businesses, events, places and incidents are either the product of the author's imagination or are used fictitiously. Any resemblance to actual events or persons, living or dead is entirely coincidental.

Copyright © 2017 Craig Hamm

All Rights Reserved. No part of this eBook may be reproduced, or stored in a retrieval system, or transmitted in any form or by any means, electronic or mechanical, including photocopying, recording, or otherwise, without express permission in writing by the author. For permission requests, email:

craighamm.author@gmail.com

I tell you, we are here on Earth to fart around, and don't let anybody tell you different.

Kurt Vonnegut - *A Man Without a Country*

# Chapter 1

Hugh had a belt round his neck when he opened the door to Kenny. It was looped through the buckle and pulled tight like a choker. Kenny wasn't sure what to say about it, so he said nothing.

"Are you coming for a pint?"

"Yeah, okay," said Hugh, stepping out of the house and closing the door behind him. He took off the belt and put in on his jeans as they walked.

"That hurts," he said, rubbing his neck.

"It can be dangerous you know."

"Of course it is."

"Was it any good?" Kenny clenched his fist and shook it as if he was masturbating.

"Oh, right. No, it was nothing like that. I was trying to kill myself."

Kenny laughed, "You had me worried for a moment there."

Thirty minutes earlier Hugh, Shagger to all who knew him, had decided that he had had enough of life and all that it had to offer him. He made the decision to try and kill himself. He was, however, only going to try. He had no intention of succeeding. The idea was to go as close as he could to the edge and see how it made him feel. He had a vague notion that his life would flash before him and that he would then find, amongst the trail of memories, a long-forgotten reason to go on, something which would give him both direction and enthusiasm. He made a noose out of a belt, placed it around his neck and threw the end over the top of the living room door. He then shut the door to keep the belt in place and, by relaxing down off his toes, tightened the noose. Unfortunately, Hugh only had two belts. The better of the two was leather and had a large eagle motif as a buckle. This had a hook for securing the belt, which made it impossible to create a self-tightening noose. The other belt was a cheap plastic one which had come free with a pair of black polyester trousers that he bought for a funeral.

As he relaxed down off his toes, the main flaw in his plan became apparent. The belt stretched with the weight of Hugh's body. The noose did tighten enough to partially restrict his breathing, but he was in no danger of having to pull back from the brink of death.

As Hugh stood there, deflated by the situation, his attention drifted to the TV in the corner. Hugh's TV was switched on in the morning and stayed on all day, whether he was watching or not. The TV was treated very much like a radio, on in the background with Hugh dipping in and out of programs. Some daytime magazine show was on. It was presented by an ex-children's TV presenter. He had replaced another ex-children's presenter who had been sacked after it had been revealed he was having a cocaine-fuelled affair with his fiancé's mother.

This presenter was either gay or sexless, which pretty much amounted to the same thing as far as Hugh was concerned. He was interviewing a woman who taught pole dancing as a fitness activity. She was dressed in a diamante-studded bikini, and he was interviewing her with no more excitement than he'd shown with the previous guest, a grandmother who had just completed her fifth charity walk to Machu Picchu.

The recent history of daytime TV was flashing before Hugh's eyes. Daytime TV was his recent life. At that moment, he heard someone at the door. It was almost 11:00 a.m. It would be Kenny looking to go for a drink. Hugh pulled the door forward to release the belt and ended his suicide bid.

***

Rob was woken by his dream. In it he was frantically searching for a toilet. Every so often he would find one and begin to urinate. He would then realise it wasn't a toilet. As was always the case when he had this kind of dream, he was vaguely aware that he was asleep and woke up wondering if he had wet himself. Rob felt the sheet he was lying on and was glad to find no damp patches. He got out of bed and made his way to the toilet. It felt good to finally relieve himself after so many frustrating attempts. Looking in the mirror he saw puffy eyes and dishevelled hair. No drink tonight, he decided. He was glad Lisa was at work. By the time she came back he would be respectable looking, and he wouldn't have to endure another lecture. He shuffled his way downstairs and poured himself a bowl of Sugar Puffs, emptied the remains of the coffee machine into a cup and heated it in the microwave. Sitting at the breakfast bar he flicked on the TV.

Rob thought about the previous night and shook his head. Everything was a fight these days, from what to have for dinner, down to what time they went to bed. Rob didn't see why they had to go to bed at the same time, but Lisa felt as though he was undermining her career by staying up to watch a movie.

"I'll keep the sound down," he'd said.

"But I'll know you're up."

"And?"

"If we're a team we should do things together."

"Fair enough, Lisa, I shouldn't have had a Pot Noodle for dinner before you came in, but sleeping isn't really in the same category. Once you're asleep, you're asleep. It's not really doing something."

"I'm working tomorrow."

"I'm not."

"Exactly, you don't work, you don't do anything. Where's the future in that?"

And that, he had concluded, was the problem. Why do busy people get so annoyed by other people doing nothing?

In the cold light of day, he admitted to himself that he had drunk more than he should have. Just before heading off to bed he had taken down the gold discs from the wall of the media room. It had been Lisa's idea to put them up and Rob had never been comfortable with them. He felt it was gaudy and boastful. He was embarrassed to have people in the room as a result, which irritated him.

Rob's review of the previous night was interrupted by a mobile phone advert on TV. A man and a woman appeared on a split screen. He walked through cold grey streets of a British town, she walked in sunshine. The two scenes merged in the middle with them holding hands. They both held mobile phones and talked and laughed with each other. The soundtrack was a simple keyboard accompaniment and Rob singing.

> *I can still hear your voice from five thousand miles away,*
>
> *I can hear the sound of rain on a warm summer day,*
>
> *The line from Johannesburg is absolutely clear,*
>
> *But all I keep thinking is I wish that you were here.*

Rob hit the breakfast bar with his middle finger. "Ka-ching," he said out loud. "I am working even when I'm not."

Four years after it had appeared on the band's last album, the song was making him money all over again. I've got a great future behind me, he thought. Pleased with the line, he stored it away for his next argument with Lisa.

***

Pitside Social Club was deserted. Apart from a couple of guys playing snooker, Hugh and Kenny were the only customers.

"You coming to the committee meeting tonight?" Andy, the bar manager, asked Hugh.

"Yeah, I suppose so."

"Another drink?"

"One more and then we'll go."

"And there was nothing then?"

"Not a thing. My mind was a blank."

"Maybe you just haven't done enough," said Andy as he poured the pints.

"You're right. I've no job, no prospects and not much of a past."

"You ever thought of getting a job?" Andy asked this question to as many people as he could. Working in Pitside Social Club consisted of mixing with a group of people who for the most part had never worked a day in their lives. Despite this fact, most of them complained about their lot. What did they expect? Why did they think that the state owed them a better quality of unemployment? It was understandable two generations back when Pitside Colliery had closed. The village was abandoned without hope of any replacement employment. No new factories or office blocks were ever going to be built in the middle of a Lanarkshire moor that looked like a moonscape on a good day. But now, two generations later, what were people waiting for? The local council had put on a subsidised bus service to Hamilton in the hope that Pitside would become a commuter village. After a few years of running empty Hamilton buses, they had put on a Glasgow service, deciding that there were more opportunities there. This, however, was no more of a success than the first service, and now two buses ran in and out of Pitside every day, only occasionally troubled by paying customers. So, Andy's quest to ask everyone in Pitside if they had ever thought of getting a job continued. It made no difference and had become a kind of catchphrase that everyone took as a joke.

"Joking aside," said Hugh, "I've got to start a 'Back into Employment' training course tomorrow. If I don't go, my benefits get cut.'

"So, that's why you tried to kill yourself," said Kenny.

They all laughed.

"Right, what are we doing next?"

"Dunno. What do you think?"

"Not sure."

Andy retreated to the storeroom to change a beer barrel. The sound of two Pitsiders trying to work out what to do with their time was more than he could bear. By the time he had finished and come back through to the bar they were still at it.

"Do you want to go down to the headless virgin?" said Hugh.

"You won't be able to vandalise it," said Andy. "It's much better protected now."

"Oh really."

"Yeah, but why don't you take that as a challenge?"

"Let's go, Kenny."

\*\*\*

The grotto of Mary's Junction had been a target of vandalism soon after it had been completed in the 1920s. The Virgin Mary at the centre of the grotto had been decapitated so many times that locals now referred to her as the headless virgin. The grotto had been built on the site of a temporary railway camp by the mainly Irish Catholic workers who were upgrading the line. When the camp had first been established there had been regular fights between the railway workers and the Protestant Pitsiders on Saturday nights. This was mostly fuelled by drink, and a Catholic priest had been called in to tend to the spiritual needs of the labourers and hopefully reduce the amount of alcohol consumed. An agreement was reached that the Pitsiders would continue to get drunk on a Saturday night, but that the railway workers would get drunk on a Sunday afternoon with their Sabbath finishing at midday. With the two communities avoiding being drunk at the same time they no longer clashed on a large scale.

This, however, left the railway workers with nothing to do on a Saturday. It was then that the priest came up with the idea of building a grotto. After working all week with railway sleepers and digging foundations, the grotto was a welcome relief. It soon became a genuine labour of love for many of the workers and its fame quickly spread. The Sunday morning mass began to attract worshippers from miles around. The camp, being temporary, had no name. Keen to avoid further conflict with the local community, the priest did not want to call it 'Pitside Grotto', so he renamed the nearby railway junction, the only other landmark, 'Mary's Junction'.

The problem the grotto faced after the camp was dismantled was that there were no longer one hundred Irish labourers to protect it and a long history of vandalism began, with decapitation of the virgin a favourite pastime for the local Protestant community.

Kenny and Hugh stood staring at the perspex box the Virgin Mary was now safely protected within.

"When did they do that?" said Hugh, not expecting any kind of an answer.

"Must have cost a fortune. Look, they've got lights as well. She must get lit up at night."

"What a waste of money." Hugh hurled a rock and watched it bounce off the transparent wall. "I hope it was the RCs that paid for it and not the council."

"It's not the same."

They sat on the dry-stone wall admiring the strength of the construction as they lobbed a few more stones at it.

"Let's go."

"End of an era," said Kenny as they made their way back along the road back to Pitside.

The London to Glasgow train passed over the nearby junction, drowning out their conversation momentarily as the clouds opened and it began to rain.

***

As Rob entered the restaurant, he could see Scott seated at a table in the internal courtyard between a giant cheese plant and a mural depicting sloth. It was one of a series throughout the restaurant representing the seven deadly sins.

"Hi Rob," Scott shouted and waved.

"Alright, Scott," Rob sat down.

Scott noticed a few of the other customers looking over. He could spot the look a mile away. They had recognised either him or Rob, probably Rob, but couldn't quite figure out where from. Scott smiled over at them.

"How's the job going, Scott?"

"Loving it. Getting to watch top quality football, talk about it and being paid for the pleasure, fantastic."

"Top quality football? I thought it was the Scottish league that you're covering?"

Scott laughed. "Okay, okay. You know what I mean. It's amazing though, isn't it? Me ending up working at the same station as Lisa."

"Crazy."

"It's a different life, but it's great."

"It's good to move on, Scott. You've done well for yourself."

"Listen, I was thinking. What about us all doing a small set at Jack's opening night? It wouldn't need much practice. We could do it with our eyes closed. I think Jack would love it and it would be great publicity for him."

Before Rob could answer Jack appeared.

"Jack are you going to be late for your own opening?" said Rob. "Remind me, it was you that invited us out for lunch, wasn't it?"

"I know, sorry. Things are kind of hectic."

"Right, let's eat," Rob handed Jack the menu.

*Ayrshire Wedges*

*Organically grown Ayrshire Potatoes. Scrubbed, chipped and cooked in a blend of extra virgin olive oil and hormone free Aberdeen Angus beef fat.*

*Pollo Parma*

*Corn fed, free range Perthshire Chicken breasts, wrapped in Parma Ham and pan fried.*

"I'll have the chicken and chips," said Rob when the waiter appeared to take their orders.

Jack smiled. "Make that two.

"I hope your menu isn't going to be as pretentious," said Rob after the waiter had left.

"By the way. I have two more footballers coming to the opening, so that is my table full."

"That's great Scott. I really appreciate the effort you've gone to. What about Lisa?" he asked Rob.

"Oh yeah, she'll be there too," said Scott, before Rob had a chance to answer.

"Good. I guess I just need to get the fixtures and fittings in place, and we should have a good night."

"I was just saying to Rob before you arrived, we should do a set at the opening, just the three of us."

"I'll be too busy on the night, Scott. I've got a band organised though. They do covers, that kind of thing, but they're very good. I've seen them play."

"Yeah but ..." Scott was interrupted by a tap on the shoulder.

"Do you do Football Night?" asked one of the customers he'd smiled at earlier.

"Yeah, that's right."

"I thought it was you. Could you give me an autograph for my son?"

"No problem," beamed Scott. "No problem at all."

He could barely contain his excitement. Here he was out with Rob, and someone was asking for his autograph, not Rob's. Not both, but only Scott's. Fantastic, Scott completely forgot about the band as he asked the man what his son's name was.

***

After lunch Rob decided that he had better walk off the booze and strolled over to the Botanical Gardens. He bought a coffee from the stall at the entrance and went into one of the greenhouses. Rob walked over to the pond near the entrance. It was stocked with unusually large goldfish. A mother was standing holding her young daughter as she peered over the railing into the water.

"What age must they be to get to that size?"

The woman smiled but didn't answer. Rob continued into the main part of the greenhouse. A tramp was sitting on one of the benches.

"Beautiful flowers," said the tramp pointing at a banana tree. He was quite clearly drunk.

Rob cupped his hand and breathed out. He could smell the booze and thought about how he looked. He had just thrown some clothes on and hadn't bothered to even fix his hair or wash.

"It's a banana tree," he replied at last, deciding not to jump to any conclusions of his own.

"Who are you? Jacques fucking Cousteau?"

"Jacques Cousteau was a marine biologist."

"Fuck off."

Rob was about to answer when he noticed the woman and child had entered the main section and were walking towards them. She stopped, hesitating. Rob smiled at her and watched as she turned round and left.

A park keeper appeared from the entrance. "Right, both of you out," he shouted.

Rob shook his head in disbelief. As he walked back past the pond, he saw the woman and child standing to one side, presumably waiting for the greenhouse to be cleared of drunks before she ventured back in. I'm not like that other guy, he wanted to tell her. I've just been to Omni for lunch. The booze you can smell is an expensive red wine. Rob smiled at the thought of it. The woman looked concerned and Rob started to laugh as he left.

Rob thought about his drinking as he walked home. He had been the only one to take a drink at lunch. Jack was heading back to his restaurant to oversee the final fittings and Scott was presenting a football highlights show later that evening. Rob, on the other hand was hanging out. Yeah, he was drinking too much, but it was just because he was between projects. He rarely got really drunk and he enjoyed the feeling of being slightly inebriated. He would, however, need to start a new project soon. He had been drifting for too long now.

When he got home, Rob looked out his boxes of graphic novels.

Lisa didn't like them being on the bookcase, so he kept them in cardboard boxes in the hall cupboard. He searched through the boxes till he came across Orpheus Jones. It was written by a local guy, Frank McCusker. Rob had met him a few times. They had expressed admiration for each other's work, as people do, but Rob meant it and he got the feeling that Frank did too. He certainly knew a lot about the band and their albums. As far as Rob was concerned Orpheus Jones was Frank's best work. It was like all good graphic novels, highly derivative with flashes of originality. It was the story of a character, Orpheus, whose girlfriend, Izzi, is killed in an explosion on the London Underground. The body was never recovered, and Orpheus comes to believe she is still alive within or below the underground. It was the mythical story of Orpheus mixed with Japanese mythology and recent political events. It was the story of someone who wanted to recover the past. Rob loved it.

He made a pot of coffee and took it through to the cinema room. He sat back on his Lazy Boy chair and lost himself in the book. A perfect afternoon lay ahead.

***

Armando was the only Catholic in Pitside. He did not live in the village but spent so much time there that he might as well. Armando owned the Golden Fry fish and chip shop. As it was the one and only fast food shop in the village, he made a good living from it. This made it all worthwhile. It compensated for the barrage of comments made by customers every time Celtic lost a football match. Armando had noticed over the years just how much business increased at dinner time on a Saturday if Celtic had lost their afternoon match. Whenever Rangers beat Celtic the shop was literally queued out of the door. The comments were never aggressive, and Armando did not feel threatened, but they were relentless. It did, however, pay for an annual six-week holiday back home to the village of Barga in Tuscany. It had also helped Armando build up a tidy nest-egg for the future. He considered himself lucky. He had several friends who had left the chip shop business in recent years. The growth of fast food chains had hit them hard and there just wasn't the same money in it anymore.

Pitside, however, was too small to ever attract a McDonalds or KFC and Armando knew he could deep fat fry for as long as he chose to. Armando planned to work until he was fifty-five and then retire to Italy. His son was not going to go into the business. He worked for a bank in Edinburgh and had no intention of swapping that for a Pitside chippy. Armando intended to rent out the shop and had a young cousin who had expressed an interest. He only had two years left and that helped keep him going, that and the constant innovation. A few years ago, deep fried pizza seemed like the limit of where you could go. Then a newspaper reported a chip shop in Glasgow that covered Mars bars in batter and deep fried them. Soon Armando started getting requests for them. He thought it would be a craze that died down after a while, but they were still as popular as ever and he had now put a Mars bar supper, deep fried Mars bar and chips, on his menu board. Another favourite was a chip supper, chips with chips. In other words, an extra-large bag of chips, but Armando thought a chip supper sounded better.

Kenny and Hugh entered the shop, drenched by the rain. Neither one with a jacket on.

"What can I get you lads?"

They shook themselves down like a couple of dogs coming out of a pond.

Kenny looked up at the menu. "I'll have a chip supper, a steak pie supper and a sausage supper."

"What are you after tonight, Shagger?"

"What's new?"

Armando turned and looked at the shelves. He turned back to face Hugh. "How about a Curly Wurly Supper?"

"A Curly Wurly Supper! Nice one. Think I'll stick to fish and chips though."

"Fair enough," Hugh never went for any of Armando's specials. He always ordered fish and chips but liked to challenge Armando to tempt him with something new.

"When are you off to Italy then, Armando?"

"Not till July."

"Must be nice getting away from here," said Hugh as he continued to shake the rain from his hair.

"It's good to get a break, but I love my job."

"Sure. Hearing the same jokes every night."

"I can't complain, Shagger. I tell the same jokes every night, don't I?"

"True."

After they left the shop Armando took down a Curly Wurly from the shelves and opened it. He turned it over several times, examining it. The lattice shape of chocolate-covered toffee would hold the batter well. It could work. He dipped it in the batter mix and brought it out. Yes, it would work. Armando dropped it into the deep fat fryer and waited for it to turn golden brown.

***

Shona watched as Kenny strolled up the path with Hugh.

"The hunter has returned," he shouted as he came through the door. Kenny came into the living room and dropped the bundle of food, wrapped in layers of paper, on the table. "Dinner is served."

"Do you really think we've been sitting here waiting for you to come home with a bag of chips? We've eaten thanks very much."

"Fair enough. All the more for me."

"What did you get?"

"Chip supper for me, Steak pie supper for you and a sausage supper for Colin."

"Well, I suppose there's no point in it going to waste. Sit down, Shagger, and I'll put the kettle on."

"Keeps saying she's going on a diet," Kenny said after she left the room. "And then she eats this lot."

"Maybe you shouldn't have got it for her then."

"Are you kidding? If I didn't, she'd have eaten half of mine. Her idea of cutting back is washing a pie supper down with a can of diet coke."

Hugh laughed. Shona hadn't aged well, but then again neither had Kenny.

Shona appeared from the kitchen. "Is he slagging me off?"

"Course not, darling."

"I know you were. You shouldn't do that in front of people. It's not right."

"You were in the kitchen."

"I mean in front of Shagger you halfwit."

"He doesn't mind. Do you, Shagger?"

Shona laughed but slapped him across the head as she passed him. "Cheeky bastard." She shouted upstairs to Colin. "Your dad's bought you a sausage supper."

"No thanks," came the reply.

"Right," said Shona as she sat down. "Does anyone want some extra chips and I'll take the sausage."

Kenny winked over at Hugh who was trying to avoid eye contact.

"Where did you two losers go today?"

"Just down the club."

"You didn't get soaked walking back from there."

"Well, we took a walk down to the grotto and got caught in the rain on the way back."

"I'll bet you didn't tell Armando you were vandalising the grotto."

"We didn't smash it up."

"It's got all sorts of protection now," said Hugh. "We couldn't get near it."

"Good. It's about time you two grew up."

Hugh finished his dinner and left to head back down to the club for the committee meeting.

"I wish you wouldn't hang around with him so much."

"Do you know he tried to kill himself today," said Kenny. "Seriously, he did. He needed a bit of company."

"How come he didn't succeed?"

"Don't be like that."

"Well, come on. How many people try and kill themselves and then just go for pint and a fish supper instead?"

"Anyway, who else would I hang out with in Pitside?"

"There's a wee guy called Colin upstairs. He quite likes football."

"It's been raining."

"On his PlayStation. Fifa World Cup."

"Aw Christ, Shona." Kenny reluctantly dragged himself out of his seat and headed upstairs.

***

Lisa's favourite film was *A Star Is Born*. In fact, her favourite films were *A Star Is born*. The 1954 version with James Mason and Judy Garland was her favourite of the three. She had seen the Barbara Streisand and Kris Kristofferson movie first and loved it, but the Garland version was hard to beat. She had, of course, also made a point of seeing the original 1937 film with Frederick March which was good, but the weakest of the three.

After Lisa first got together with Rob, she had indulged herself in fantasies that pretty much followed the pattern of the movie. Rob had already broken up the band and despite doing a couple of things since he had pretty much given up. Lisa meanwhile had been slowly building up a TV career. She had started as a junior reporter and was now the lunchtime entertainment anchor on the Scottish news. What's more she'd managed to get a few slots on a network holiday program which had led to her own cable TV show. Now she was in the running to present a new network daytime show, Doghouse Makeover. The idea of the show was to do a house makeover for dog lovers whose homes had been wrecked by their pets. There were three people short-listed for the show - Lisa, a weather girl, and a former Miss Great Britain who was married to a footballer.

If she could pull off the job, she would be living the movie. He was a declining star, she was rising. Of course, it couldn't last, she knew that, they were constantly arguing. As cruel as it sounded, though, she would like to hit the big time before they split up. It might not be the romantic view of the movie, but that is what happened in it. The rising star was helped on her way by her partner before he crashed and burned. Rob had not opened any doors for Lisa as such, but he had made her more interesting in many people's eyes. When she got a mention in TV World magazine she was introduced as holiday presenter and Rob's girlfriend. He had been a national figure and to some extent he still was, although his fame was fading fast.

Lisa was aware of her own cynicism and was untroubled by it. She had put a lot of effort into Rob. She had tried to steer him back to the music business, tried to motivate him. He had done a soundtrack for some low-budget movie, but that was it. If he didn't take the opportunities when they came along there wasn't much else she could do. It was a source of regret. A bittersweet regret, but regret, nonetheless.

Now she stood at the door of the cinema room looking at him. He was asleep in his recliner chair with a comic on his lap. A comic, this did not happen with Frederick March. It did not happen with James Mason. It did not happen with Kris Kristofferson. A fucking comic.

Where was the tragic dignity in that? True, he had taken all his gold discs down off the walls, which was kind of sad, but to sit there with a half-drunk pot of coffee, a plate with the empty silver wrappers from some chocolate biscuits and some kind of comic book on his lap. This was not the stuff of dreams.

Rob woke up, yawned and noticed Lisa standing, staring at the doorway.

"Hi honey, how was your day?"

"Fine, how was yours?"

"Yeah good, I met up with Jack and Scott for lunch."

"Scott told me. What's that you're reading?"

"Oh," he sat up animated. "Orpheus Jones. You remember Frank McCusker?"

"Not really," she said cutting him off. "What do you want for dinner?"

"Why don't I head down to Byres Road and bring us both back a Chinese carry-out?"

"Whatever." As soon as Doghouse Makeover comes through, that's it, she decided.

***

Committee meetings at the Pitside Social Club had been well attended since the decision was taken to give each committee member two complimentary drinks per meeting.

Andy brought over a tray of Pitside Zombies, a cocktail designed by the committee to make the most of their free drink allocation.

"Thanks Andy," said the chairman. "Can we just start with the management update since you're here?"

"Sure." He sat down. "Well, employment remains very low in the village which affects the level of disposal income. Combine that with the fact that most under-twenty-fives are not coming into the club due to their preference for illegal drugs, and the trading position continues to be poor and declining."

Everyone laughed.

"So," said the chairman. "I take it you mean we're not doing very well at the moment?"

"Pish."

"And it's getting worse?"

"It's as pish as I can remember."

"Any suggestions?"

"Either more people need to get jobs so that they have more money to spend, we need to start selling illegal drugs, or the government needs to win the war against narcotics and young people start using alcohol again as the main way to get wasted."

"Any sensible suggestions?" asked the chairman.

"Not from me. I better get back to the bar. Give me a shout when you want another drink."

"Anyone else got any suggestions?" the chairmen looked around the committee.

"Events," said Hugh. "We need to put on more events."

"What kind of events do you mean, Shagger?"

"Anything and everything."

"What, like fundraisers for the United Ulster Force?" said another committee member. "We only took £300 over the bar at the last one and we raised even less on the door."

"Well no wonder," someone else added. "What do they need a United Ulster Force for anyway? There's peace in Ireland. It's a joke, the whole thing. Do you know how many tickets we've sold for the next one? Ten. At that rate the bar won't even pay for itself."

"Ten tickets? I didn't realise it was that bad." Hugh felt a wave of nausea.

"Why would anyone want to go? It's just paying to get into your own club."

"We could try and book a Karaoke," said Hugh. "That's always popular."

"Well, you're not getting an advance from club funds. You'll need to fund it out of the ticket sales."

"Look, I know these things aren't as popular as they used to be. Less people have been turning up every time. But we can't just cancel it. What would I say to Jaffa?"

"You could tell him to use some of the money he makes selling drugs. That's assuming he ever gives the UUF the money he gets from the fundraisers."

There was a murmur of approval from the committee.

"Do any of you want to tell him that?" Hugh glanced round the table at the members. There was silence. "Well, I'll tell him that this will be the last fundraiser, but that's as far as I'm willing to go."

"Right, onto the formal business," said the chairman, keen to move on from talk of Jaffa. "First up, air fresheners. As you all know the smoking ban has had its effect on the place. Without smoke to cover all the other smells, the place is stinking. We've had a company in who rent automatic scent dispensers. They're installing the units next week, but we need to decide on the smell. There's five choices …"

Hugh drifted off, thinking about Jafffa. How the hell was he going to tell him? The guy was a psychopath and Hugh already owed him £500. He was on track for a severe beating. He'd seen what Jaffa was capable of.

"Shagger. What do you think?" asked the chairman.

"Sorry, about what?"

"Cucumber Fresh or Citrus Orange?"

***

Rob was watching *Hitler in Colour* on the Discovery Channel and drinking a beer when Lisa came through with a coffee for him.

"Did you remember?"

"Sure, what channel's it on?" he asked.

"456"

"Wow, there's so many now isn't there?" Rob flicked to the correct channel.

"I wish you wouldn't drink every night."

"I know." His good intentions had quickly drifted after the Chinese meal. It just seemed to demand a cold beer to wash it down. "It's only one and it is the last one for tonight."

"Good. Are you looking forward to this?"

"Sure."

"Why did you take down the gold discs last night?"

"I just don't think they fit the room."

"You know, Rob, I still believe in you. You just have to fight for it if you want it."

"Are you talking about music?"

"Maybe it was easier when you were younger, but you can still do it. You just have to work harder."

Rob sighed but answered anyway. "I don't think the music business is like that, Lisa. The stuff that is made without effort is usually the best. People's ability usually peaks quite early on in their career. I don't say that out of bitterness. It's just a fact."

"Don't give up, Rob."

"I haven't. I've just moved on. I was very happy with the work I did on the Rose Garden soundtrack."

"It was good but, well, I mean you can't listen to a soundtrack on its own, can you?"

"Tell that to Michael Nyman."

"Who?"

"*The Piano*. Anyway, that's not really the main point of a soundtrack"

"Oh, look, it's starting, shh!"

Lisa appeared on the screen in front of the Eiffel Tower. "Hi, I'm Lisa Ward and I'm inviting you to take a road trip with me through France. We'll visit some well-known places like … well, the Eiffel Tower. But we'll also visit some places off the beaten track, so sit back, relax and join me in France *avec* Ward."

The music began and the opening credits rolled.

"It's clever isn't it, France *avec* Ward."

"Very."

They sat back and watched the program. Lisa visited every picture postcard scene imaginable. Rob wondered to himself when they were getting off the beaten track. Each small town they visited turned into a history lesson. What minor French historical figure had been born there. What food came from there, what happened during the German occupation, what films had been made.

"Look, Rob, this next village is beautiful. It's where they filmed *Jamon des Sources*."

"You mean *Mannon des Sources*?"

"Yes, you knew what I meant."

On the screen, Lisa stood in a village street. "I'm in the town of Ansouis. If this scene looks more than a little familiar to you, you might just be recognising it from that wonderful film, *Mannon des Sources*."

Rob laughed.

"What?"

"I was just imagining that you'd said *Jamon des Sources* on camera. The source of ham. The tale of an innocent pig farmer struggling against the vested interests of a patriarchal village."

"Very funny."

"Sorry," said Rob squeezing her arm. "It's good."

The program dragged on through half a dozen other beautiful villages.

"Look, I'm about to play your music."

On screen, Lisa was standing against her car at a vantage point overlooking the Cote d'Azur.

"Well, I'm nearing the end of my journey and soon it will be time to head home. I've missed home and I've missed Rob, but I have one last journey to make. The beautiful Cote d'Azur behind me. Home will have to wait just a little while longer. And besides, when you live with a musician, he's never that far away."

The scene cut to Lisa driving again. She flicked on the radio and '5000 miles' came on.

*I can still hear your voice from 5000 miles away,*

*I can hear the sound of rain on a warm summer day,*

"You do realise that I will get paid for that?" said Rob.

"I know. But it was the producer's idea, not mine. And this was made before the phone advert. So, there's nothing to feel guilty about."

"I don't. I just wondered if you realised. That's all."

"Yes, of course I did."

"I have a great future behind me."

"Don't be sad," Lisa kissed him on the cheek. Two careers passing in different directions on the very program she made. Lisa had a feeling of life making sense again.

Rob shook his head. Maybe it wasn't such a great line after all.

***

Hugh found Jaffa sitting in his living room when he came back from the meeting. Jaffa had made himself a cup of tea and was reading an old newspaper.

"Christ, you gave me a fright."

"Hope you don't mind me making myself at home?"

"No."

"Good, sit down, Shagger."

"Thank you," said Hugh, without knowing why. He sat down.

"How's the fundraiser tickets going?"

"Not very well, Jaffa."

"That's a pity. Remind me, how much did the last night raise?"

"About £200 in ticket sales. The bar only took £300 that night."

"No, how much did it raise? Not how much money did it take in."

"£200."

Jaffa sighed. Like jokes, the impact of threats was diluted when you had to explain them. "Shagger, how much money am I due from the last fundraiser?"

"Oh right, £500."

"So, I'm thinking to myself that you were looking to catch up with this next fundraiser. Make up for lost ground. Am I right?"

"Yeah, I guess."

"How many tickets have you sold?"

"Ten," said Hugh. He knew there was no point in lying. Jaffa did not make pointless visits. He obviously knew already.

"That's £50 so far."

"It's getting harder to sell them now that there's peace." Hugh bit the bullet. "People don't see the point in the fundraising anymore."

"What do you think we should do then?"

"To be honest, I think we should take a break from it. It could get embarrassing if we keep doing them and less and less people turn up."

"Do you know what embarrasses me?"

"What?" asked Hugh, already knowing the answer.

"It embarrasses me when people who owe me money don't pay up. It affects my business, because other people think that they can get away with it."

"Don't worry, Jaffa, I will get you the £500."

"I'm not worried. I'm concerned. You see, your deadline is the next fundraiser and it's not looking too good. I like to be organised. I like to anticipate problems and then prevent them."

"I will pay up."

"I do take your point about the fundraisers though. Let's make this next one the last for a while."

"Really. Great. I think it's the right thing to do."

"But let's make sure it goes out with a bang. Plenty of people. A good night."

"I was thinking of organising a Karaoke to boost the numbers."

"Sounds good. Tell you what, you can keep any surplus we make above £500. In fact, you give me £500 and then keep any money raised from the night. How does that sound?"

Hugh had reached the same arrangement the last time round with dire consequences. The night had raised only £200 and now he owed Jaffa £500.

"I think I would rather go back to the normal arrangement."

"Well, there's a bit of a problem with that, Shagger. You see you don't have any source of income and therefore they only way you could pay me back is by stealing money from the next fundraiser. Do you see that?"

"Well …"

"This way you can do it honestly. Work your arse off selling tickets and you can pay me what you owe me without stealing. So, it's agreed?"

"Okay," said Hugh, realising that it was not open to discussion.

"So, to clarify. You owe me £500 from the last fundraiser and you will pay me £500 from the next one. So, you owe me £1000."

"Right."

"Don't look so depressed. It is possible. Sell 100 tickets, have a few raffles and you've made £1000. Debt paid in full. I'm not looking for you to fail. I'm just encouraging you to succeed."

After Jaffa left, Hugh poured himself a drink and switched on the TV. A thousand pounds might as well be a million pounds. It was beyond his ability to raise that amount. Hugh couldn't even remember whose idea it was the last time for him to 'buy' the fundraiser. As for the £200 he made, Hugh wasn't sure what he'd spent the money on. It all just disappeared over a four-week period. He and Kenny had a good time, but not that good. Hugh's attention drifted to the TV. The phone-in quiz had just started. One pound per call and a top prize of £10,000. Hugh was only briefly tempted, remembering the all-night session he and Kenny had, drinking and phoning in to the quiz. They didn't get on air once and had spent £50 by the time they gave up.

The phone rang. It was Hugh's mother phoning to let him know that his uncle had died and when the funeral was. Hugh's hands were shaking when he came off the phone. It wasn't grief. He didn't remember the uncle at first. For Hugh it seemed like a sign. Jaffa had never actually killed anyone for not paying a debt, but Hugh knew that he would inflict a permanent injury on him. Hugh would be branded for life. A walking advert for Jaffa and, somehow, not fully himself. He knew because he'd seen others in the same position.

The TV quiz was asking for the name of five films with the word 'star' in the title. Star Wars thought Hugh. It had to be. If he thought he'd any chance of getting through, he would call. The first caller came on and said Star Wars. The bubbly presenter shook her head, said no and smiled. Crazy, thought Hugh. It had to be Star Wars. He poured himself another drink and racked his brain for another film with 'star' in the title.

\*\*\*

Rob's father phoned to let him know about his uncle's death. Rob was not that close to his uncle but knew that non-attendance was not an option. In his father's eyes that would be Rob letting the side down and worse still would be blamed on his fame. Rob confirmed his mandatory attendance and said goodnight to his father. He then went through to the kitchen and got a beer. Lisa had gone to bed early and happy after France *avec* Ward. She would never know if he just had another one. Rob began to look on the bright side. He would see some cousins that he hadn't met for a few years. Raymond would be there, obviously, it was his father who had died. Hugh might turn up, he was always good for a laugh. Alison and Brenda too, yeah, it should be good. Rob couldn't help himself, but he was starting to look forward to the funeral.

\*\*\*

Jaffa put on his *Rat Pack Live at the Sands* CD as he made the short drive home. Frank Sinatra, Dean Martin and Sammy Davis Junior swapped insults and slaughtered half the songs they sung, but it was all part of the atmosphere of the album. The laughter of the audience could be heard, and Jaffa imagined himself back in the 1960's Las Vegas casino. A world away from Pitside and petty debts. A grand was a grand though and Shagger would find the money from somewhere. A relative or friend, or a combination of the two, would save his skin. Besides, Jaffa had problems of his own.

Ever since the Good Friday peace deal had been signed in Northern Ireland, Jaffa felt as though he was living on borrowed time. As a member of the U.U.F. he had been untouchable. As soon as peace broke out, so too did several internal feuds within the organisation. One group had fled Northern Ireland completely and Jaffa had found himself giving lodgings to a psychopath and his only slightly less-deranged wife for several weeks. Eventually they left for

Yorkshire to start an illegal business selling duty free booze and cigarettes.

Jaffa continued with his own business which consisted of drugs, cigarettes, pirate DVDs and acting as a loan shark to the five local villages. All the while, though, Jaffa was waiting for one of two things to happen. Some Glasgow-based gang would move in to his patch, no longer worried by his ability to call on paramilitary colleagues from Belfast to come his aid, or more likely, another group of U.U.F. members would flee Ulster and one of them would decide to take over Jaffa's business. The five villages were effectively a U.U.F. franchise and if someone more powerful wanted to, they could take it off him. Jaffa was not rich, but it was a cash business and he did well enough. Besides, he didn't know anything else.

All the locals saw was a tough, no-nonsense kind of guy who told them what to do and expected it to be done. They didn't see the pressures and stresses that he had to deal with. Their lives would be the same today, tomorrow, next week and next year. Jaffa simply didn't know what was around the corner.

No, the more he thought about it, Shagger had it easy, even if he had never wanted to buy either of the fundraising nights. What Shagger didn't realise was that no matter how bad things seem, there is always someone worse off than yourself.

On the CD Frank sang to Dean:

'If I had a hammer'

Instead of following it up with 'I'd hammer in the morning', he sang:

'I'd smash you in the mouth'

The audience roared with laughter and Jaffa laughed along with them. Classic, he thought. Absolute classic.

# Chapter 2

Hugh woke up with the sound of his alarm clock buzzing. He swatted it, hitting the snooze button. He stared at the clock for a second, trying to work out why he had set it. The fog of sleep lifted, and he remembered the Back to Work course.

Hugh wasn't awake that early very often. He felt terrible. His head was thumping, and his mouth was dry. The course started at 9:30 a.m. down at the community centre. He thought about going back to sleep for half an hour but knew he would never wake up again on time. Hugh pulled his duvet around him and got up. He went downstairs, made a cup of tea and sat down in the living room to watch some TV. This would help wake him up. That was the theory at least, but Hugh found himself struggling to keep his eyes open. There obviously weren't that many people who watched TV at this time in the morning he concluded. All that was on was news. It was worse than the news at night. They dragged each item out as long as they could and seemed to have an expert available on every single subject. Hugh wondered how you become an expert, then imagined himself as one, sitting in a large waiting room crowded with experts waiting to be called.

He was snapped back awake by his tea spilling. Shit, he thought. Need to get going or I'll never make it. Hugh left his duvet where it was and went back upstairs, tea in hand.

Five minutes later he was stepping out of the house, pulling his jacket together against the cold and heading down the street. Most of the houses still had their curtains drawn. The place felt eerie at this time in the morning, deserted. Hugh looked at his watch. It was now ten past nine. He headed down to the shop since he still had some time to kill. The Golden Fry and the shop sat next to each other on Downside Street. The Golden Fry was closed, the security rollers pulled down to show the graffiti. Armando cleaned it up about once a year. In times gone by there was always at least one U.U.F. or U.D.A. logo on the shutters. Someone had even tried to paint a red hand of Ulster once, but it just came out as a huge red blob. What Hugh had noticed in the last few years was that Ulster slogans were dying out. The whole Northern Ireland thing was just not as important as it used to be, and here he was still trying to raise money off the back of it. The absence of the slogans another reminder of the trouble he was in. Hugh went into the shop and bought a can of coke and a packet of crisps.

"You're out and about early this morning," said Davy, the shopkeeper.

"I know and I'm feeling it. How come you're open already?"

"I get loads of trade from the kids heading to school. It's like a breakfast club in here in the morning."

"Right," said Hugh. "I never thought of that. Listen, has your cousin still got the Karaoke business?"

"Sure, you looking to book him?"

"Could you find out if he's free next Friday?"

Davy sucked air in through his teeth. "You'll be lucky, but I'll give him a phone this morning."

Hugh left the shop more depressed than he'd entered it. Without something to attract the punters, the fundraiser would be a disaster. Hugh looked at his watch again. It was now 9:20 a.m. He sat on the wall and ate his crisps. As he sat there, Hugh tried to think of other ways of earning some money. Nothing came to him. After finishing his crisps, he stood up and headed down to the community centre and the Back to Work course.

***

When Scott had got the job as a sports presenter it had been made clear to him that it would be better if he didn't support Rangers or Celtic. If he did, it would immediately antagonise one half of his audience. Sport in Scotland meant football and football meant Rangers and Celtic. This did not come as news to Scott. He was aware of the Old Firm stranglehold on football even though he had only ever shown a passing interest in the sport up until the point that he had applied for the job. Avoiding support for Rangers and Celtic was not a problem. The real decision to be made was which team he would support. Scott needed to build up credibility with a sports audience and the best way to do that was to show some kind of club allegiance. He had to pick a side that he could claim a connection to, but also one that would only occasionally come up against the Old Firm in a cup competition, and even then, be unceremoniously defeated. Studying the lower leagues Scott came up with the perfect solution. Stenhousemuir were a team that had never achieved anything. They were so obscure most people didn't even know where they came from. They came from Stenhousemuir, but you couldn't always rely on the name of a team. Raith Rovers, after all, came from Kirkaldy, not Raith, as some people assumed. Scott's father came from out that way before moving to Glasgow, so he had a reasonable excuse for supporting them.

Scott had been over the moon to get the job. The band had broken up two years earlier and he had finally accepted that Rob was unlikely to agree to a permanent re-forming of the Deltas. Staying in the music business was not really an option. Scott was a reasonable bass player, but not great and he did not write any of his own material.

It was a bold, if not unique, move for the TV station to take and Scott worked hard to absorb every football cliché he could prior to starting. Just before he did start, Scott was interviewed on the lunchtime news by Lisa. He knew her of course but had never appreciated how professional she was at her job. As they were being mic'd up, she carried on talking to Scott as if no-one else was there, but also making sure she said nothing too personal or revealing. "You must be aware of and ignore the civilians simultaneously," she had told him. There and then Scott decided that he wanted Lisa. She was the one for him. Was it partly because she was with Rob? He had thought about that, quickly realised that he didn't really care, and never gave it another thought. Lisa would be his sooner or later. Now time was running out. He managed to have a coffee with her most days in the station canteen, they talked and laughed and flirted. He felt the connection, he was sure of it. But now, the travel program and the Doghouse Makeover. If she got that one, she would be out of town in a flash, leaving Rob and Glasgow behind. He was sure of it. She would also, however, be leaving Scott behind. Scott would be stuck in Glasgow talking twice a week about Rangers and Celtic and pretending to support Stenhousemuir. Scott had to make his move soon.

Seeing Lisa in the canteen he quickened his step only to be cut off by Rab McBride.

"Alright, Scott?"

"Yeah fine, Rab. Just going to grab a coffee."

"I'll join you."

Scott saw Lisa disappear out of the canteen, the moment lost.

"How's the Manure? Still propping up the third division?" Rab laughed at his own joke.

After being interviewed by Lisa, Scott had been invited on to Rab's program, *Show Us Your Balls,* which was billed as a light-hearted look at football. During the interview Rab had asked Scott who he supported. He then asked Scott to repeat the name several times before having a mock Eureka moment. "Oh, you mean Stenhouse manure," he said. The audience and Rab roared with laughter. Scott realised that he should have just gone for supporting Falkirk which was only a few miles down the road from Stenhousemuir. Rab pointed out that if you drove into Stenhousemuir and then followed the road signs for football traffic, they directed you back out of town and towards Falkirk Football Club. Ever since the interview, whenever they spoke, Stenhousemuir was always asked about and referred to as 'the manure'. Walking with Rab and seeing Lisa disappear, Scott knew he had to make his move soon. Without Lisa this place and this job would be worse than meaningless.

***

As Gordon drove into Pitside he knew it wasn't going to be a good day. Immediately upon entering the village he had to make an emergency stop to avoid running over two dogs that ran across the road. The fact that no-one chased after the dogs told him everything heeded to know about Pitside. Gordon had delivered his Back to Work seminars in some of the worst areas in the west of Scotland and the number one sign of a tough day ahead was free-range dogs. Gordon worked as an independent trainer, taking many of the jobs that no-one else wanted. He was aware of the fact that everyone who came on one of his courses had been forced along, but he prided himself in trying to make them as engaging as possible and set himself private targets of turning around the perceptions of half his participants by the end of the course. The dogs told him that fifty percent would be an optimistic target today.

Arriving at the local community centre things didn't look any better. It was a modular building with damp patches where there was no graffiti. The door was still locked and even after banging on it for a few minutes there was no sign of life. Gordon looked up the mobile number the caretaker had given him.

"Sorry about that," said Bob as he opened the door. "I couldn't hear you through the back and I need to keep the door locked."

"Not a problem. I don't suppose you could give me a hand with my equipment?"

Bob looked up and down the street. "Okay, but let's make it quick."

After setting up his flipcharts and other equipment Gordon sat down with Bob for a cup of tea and listened to his tales of woe. The firebomb attacks, the smashed windows and the time he had to call a locksmith to get him out of the building after the locks had been damaged with superglue. Gordon was sure that he saw a tear welling up in Bob's eye as he recounted the story.

"Hey, let me show you something," Gordon changed the subject.

He pulled some balloons and a pump out of one of his plastic crates. He then inflated the balloons and then bent them into various shapes, a dog, a swan, a sword.

"What do you think?"

Bob shook his head. "I think they'll eat you alive."

***

After brief introductions Gordon gave his standard opening performance. He held up the dog-shaped balloon.

"What is this?" he asked.

Silence.

Gordon pointed at one of the attendees. "John, what is this?"

"It's a dog," said John.

"And this," he pointed to the next person.

"It's a bird."

"And this?"

"It's a pirate's sword," said Hugh.

"Excellent," said Gordon. Notice that none of you said it was a balloon."

"It's kind of obvious that they're balloons," said Hugh.

"Exactly, but as well as being a balloon, it can be a dog or a swan or a sword. In fact, it can be almost anything you want it to be. And that is the same as a job. You can have a job as a fireman or a shop assistant or a joiner or an actor. They are all jobs, but that's just about all they have in common. The point is that nobody really wants a job as such. They want to be a fireman or a shop assistant or a joiner or whatever. That's why I call this session of the course 'What shape is my balloon?'. It's not the balloon that kids want, it's the dog balloon or the sword balloon and that's what we're going to do today. We're going to find out what shape your balloon is." Gordon paused for effect. "Any comments or thoughts? Is this just some crazy guy talking or does some of it make sense?"

"I've never liked balloons," said Sarah. "Doesn't matter what shape they are, I just don't like balloons. The feel of them makes my skin crawl,"

"What are you going to do with the balloons?" asked John. "It's just that my son would love the sword. Would you mind if I take it home with me at the end of the day?"

***

Scott still wanted the band to get back together. Not full time, just for the occasional gig. Charity concerts ideally. Nothing too controversial. Green issues or world poverty would do. Everyone was against poverty and pretty much everyone seemed to be claiming to be an environmentalist. Scott had a vision of doing one or two concerts a year. He didn't even mind if he wasn't paid for them. He would want the costs covered of course, but other than that he didn't mind. The main thing was to stay known for his music.

He had noticed on many occasions just how much it seemed to qualify him as an interesting person, regardless of the circumstances. Footballers, who would otherwise treat him as any other hack, saw him as one of them, a fellow celebrity. A real celebrity, famous for doing something rather than just being famous. The first time he was invited to a private party by a footballer, Scott expected to see many of his fellow sports journalists. There were none. Not a single other journalist was there. It was Scott, footballers, their friends and some football groupies.

"Why did you only invite me?" Scott asked the host.

"You've done this, Scott," he said sweeping his hand around the room. "Don't tell me there weren't some wild parties when you were on tour?"

"Yeah, too many."

"You've done it, Scott. Journalists are just journalists."

And so, Scott knew how it was. If people remembered him for his music, he was a real celebrity. The moment they stopped he would be a celebrity observer. Invited to attend only when required, never for his own company.

It was, of course, possible to become a real celebrity as a high-profile TV presenter, but you had to go national for that. Scott aspired to this, but he knew that it was some time away, if ever. The net result was that he still felt dependent on Rob since the breakup. Without him there was no band. If Rob had died instead of Keith, Scott could have stepped into the front man role for the charity gigs he dreamt of. Unfortunately, it was Keith that died. A swimming accident in Majorca. Hardly rock and roll. Keith had gone on holiday after the band had finished recording an album. One morning he dived into the sea and misjudged the water depth. He hit his head on a rock and that was that. It was that random and meaningless. Afterwards they did one concert as a tribute to Keith, but Rob had refused all suggestions to get the band back together since.

"It's impossible to get the band together," Rob would say. "Keith's dead. Without him it wouldn't be the band."

It was all very well for Rob to say that. He wrote most of their songs and together with Keith was credited with all of them. He was still picking up a tidy sum in rights. There had been several cover versions, one song "Drunken Love" had been used as a theme tune to a drama series on TV, and now there was the mobile phone advert.

Meanwhile, Jack and Scott had to start over and find new careers. Scott as a TV presenter and now Jack was opening his restaurant, a glorified pizza parlour. What kind of life was that?

To cap it all off, Scott could lose Lisa if she got her big break. If it hadn't been for the repeated attempts of Scott to get the band together, he would have made his move on Lisa two years ago. Scott was sure that Rob and Lisa were completely incompatible, and it was just a matter of time before they spit up. He had thought he could wait it out and then make his move on Lisa without jeopardising the band reunion. One scenario he had imagined even helped get the band back together again. He imagined Rob and Lisa having an amicable split, agreeing to stay friends. Scott would comfort Lisa and one thing would lead to another. Scott would then go to Rob and let him know. Rob would give his blessing and promise that it wouldn't affect their friendship. Scott would then explain that Lisa was convinced it would. If Rob would agree to a charity gig it would act like a symbolic approval to Lisa. Rob would, of course, enjoy the gig and agree to make it an annual event.

Instead of this happening, Rob and Lisa were still together and acted like an old disgruntled couple who would never actually do anything about it. If Lisa got the network job, she'd be gone. It would the catalyst for them finally splitting up.

"Lisa," he shouted after her in the corridor outside the canteen.

"Oh, hi Scott."

"Do you want to meet up for lunch? I thought we could go over your program. I watched it last night. France *avec* Ward."

"Really?"

"Yeah, the canteen's fine if you're pushed for time."

"Oh no, I can't do lunch. So, you liked the program?"

Scott's face reddened. "No problem. Some other time."

"It's just that I'm meeting my agent."

"Well, if you need some moral support?"

"Rob's meeting us. But I'll catch up with you later this afternoon. I must dash. See you."

And with that she was off again. A woman on a mission. A mission that Scott wanted to be part of.

\*\*\*

"You have to hang out with people you don't like," said Hugh smiling.

The others murmured their approval.

"You guys almost finished?" asked Gordon.

"Yeah."

"Right, choose a spokesperson and re-join the main group."

Ten minutes earlier Gordon had split them into groups of four to do the 'Pros and Cons' exercise. The task was to create a list of pros and cons about working. Gordon used this exercise when his introductory talk didn't go down well. The pros and cons exercise acknowledged the negative feelings people had about work. In Gordon's experience, it was much better to accept this and move on from there.

"Right, who's going to go first?"

Silence.

"Okay Hugh, can you go over your list?"

Hugh stood up. "Right, for the pros we had the fact that you can earn more money, but there was a bit of an argument about that."

"Let's just park that one for the time being and go on with the rest of your list."

"Cons," said Hugh. "Well, I won't do all of them, but the main ones were, you need to get up early every day. That means you also need to go to bed early every night. You wouldn't have as much of a social life during the week because of that, and even at the weekend you'd be so tired that you probably wouldn't do as much. Sunday would be a right-off for a start. If you have kids like Sarah here, you couldn't be in for them coming home from school, so you'd have less family time. You'd also have to travel to and from work, so that takes up more time again. You need to hang out with people you don't like. That was the main ones. There were others, but all pretty much on the same themes."

"Well that's certainly comprehensive," said Gordon. "Was there only the one positive?"

"Yes, but as I said we had a bit of an argument about that. Although you earn money, it gets taxed, you have to pay for travel, lunch, maybe extra clothes. All these things add up and you would lose all sorts of benefits. So, you could end up having say forty quid more in your hand every week for working forty hours. In other words, you've worked for one pound an hour. That's less than the minimum wage and you've destroyed your lifestyle into the bargain. It's crazy really."

"Not only that," said another member of the group. "But if it doesn't work out and you don't like it, you can't just give it up. You wouldn't get your benefits back and you'd end up worse off than before you took the job."

Heads nodded in agreement.

"So," said Hugh. "The group was split as to whether it really was a pro or a con."

Gordon took a breath. "That assumes that you are in a fairly low-paid job."

"But the reality is that we would be. We're not going to get jobs as brain surgeons, are we?"

"No, that's true," said Gordon. "But then again, your first job is not likely to be your last."

"That's another negative," someone shouted.

Gordon faked a smile to pace the mood. "And the first job is a steppingstone to the second which is a steppingstone to the third and so on until you do end up in a job that is well paid and interesting. The poorly paid job, the uninteresting job, is part of the journey, not where you want to end up, not the destination. Is selling cigarettes and newspapers out of a kiosk well paid? No, but one man did just that fifty years ago in London till he earned enough to buy a second kiosk that someone worked in for him. He then got a third and a fourth until he was a millionaire."

Gordon pulled some sheets out of one of his folders and passed copies round the class.

"That's just one of the stories on this sheet. Every one of them true, every one of them about someone who started with nothing and made a success of themselves. They weren't all rich, one woman ended up as a professor in a subject she loved. Success can be money, or it can be just doing something you enjoy."

"What if you enjoy doing nothing?" someone asked. The group laughed.

"Let's be honest," said Hugh. "That gets a laugh, but are you happy hanging around Pitside every day doing nothing?"

"Listen to you. What have you ever done?"

"Nothing, and I don't want to go and work at some job that pays rotten money, but that doesn't mean I'm happy. It just means I don't know how to make my life any better. If you died tomorrow and your life flashed before your eyes, what would be the highlights? Are there any?"

"Of course there are."

"What are they?" Hugh asked. "Did any of them happen in the last two years or even the last five, or is it fifteen years ago when you first had sex?"

"Cheeky bugger," said Sarah.

"Okay, let's move on to the next group," said Gordon, keen to avoid any arguments before they got too heated. Must remember that, he thought. Life highlights and when they happened. It was at moments like these that Gordon loved his job. Someone challenging the consensus of the group. Someone admitting out loud, this isn't a

40

good life, it's not a good way to live. He might not reach half the people in this group, but he would get through to some of them.

"We didn't have any positives," said the next group leader. "But this is our list of negatives."

\*\*\*

Rob closed the door behind him and glanced at his watch. Twelve o'clock. He had plenty of time to get into town. Lunch was at 1:45 p.m. Lisa came off air at one, so lunch was more of a mid-afternoon snack. Rob had decided to walk into town. Staring at himself in the mirror he had concluded that he was going to seed. He had put on too much weight and even though he could sleep as long as he wanted, and often did, he also looked like someone who needed a good twelve hours. His hair was a shapeless mess and while it had never been something he'd spent time or money on, it was now out of control. At best, he thought he could be described as bohemian looking. The problem was, as he realised from his encounter in the park the previous day, there was a very thin line between bohemian and down-and-out. Rob's walk into town was part of his effort to get into shape. It would take him about an hour and depending how he felt he would also walk back. That would be two hours light exercise. Not a bad start to his new regime.

Reaching Byres Road, he went into a café and bought a takeaway latte and a biscotti. He then walked up past the university and down onto Gibson Street. This was a journey he had taken many times as a student to save a few pounds of drinking money. Rob was not a nostalgic person at all, but this area was alive with memories for him. The second-hand shops, the food takeaways mixed in with interior design and antique shops. Rob stopped at the comic book shop and looked in the window. They had a copy of Orpheus Jones in the window. He stepped into the shop and waited for the man behind the counter to look up from reading. He didn't.

"Can I have a copy of Orpheus Jones."

The shopkeeper now looked up, took a drink of his tea and said, "We're not keen on people bringing food and drink into the shop," pointing at Rob's coffee.

Rob shrugged. "Orpheus Jones," he repeated.

"I was surprised that it didn't do better. Could hardly give them away, but I thought it was his best work."

"You're right. I think it was just too raw. Too soon after the event."

"What do you mean?" asked the shopkeeper.

"People weren't ready to read fictional accounts of bombings so soon after the real thing."

"Just the one copy?" he asked, not interested in conversation that linked the comic books he sold to real life."

"Two copies thanks," said Rob.

"Well, I only have two copies. That wouldn't leave me with any."

"Yes, but the aim of a shop is to sell stuff, so that's probably a good thing." Rob explained.

"Okay," said the shopkeeper. He took the copy from the shop window and then began to search through boxes for the second copy. "It's here somewhere."

"I thought you couldn't give them away?"

"Well yeah, at first, but then they just sold in a steady stream ever since."

"So, it is quite popular?"

"Here it is," said the shopkeeper, turning around. "Sold more of this than any other book we've stocked. I guess it's just word of mouth. That's twenty-five quid. Why do you want two copies anyway?"

"The cover price is a tenner," said Rob.

"It's out of print and it's a first edition. It's collectible. Why do you want two copies?"

Rob handed over the money. "I'll keep one and sell one on Ebay. That will mean that I end up owning one that I effectively paid nothing for."

"That's not right," the shopkeeper said angrily.

"I'm joking. The second one is a present for my girlfriend. She's a big McCusker fan."

"Cool."

Rob left the shop and continued his walk. The two copies were to allow him to cut them up and still have a full copy of each picture from both sides of a page. That way, his original would still be intact. Rob felt he could do something with the story. He wasn't sure what, but he wanted to play around with it and see what emerged. It could be a set of songs or a stage production. He would simply work his way through each picture and select individual images that stood out and see what he made of them. Frank McCusker might not be interested, but it didn't matter. Rob was happy to have the beginnings of a project that he could focus on. He would work something basic up, before approaching Frank.

Rob stopped outside a hair salon to put his empty coffee cup in a bin. He looked in the window and made eye contact with one of the hairdressers who was facing out onto the street, her client's head cut off by the back of a mirror. She smiled at him and he smiled back. The face looked familiar, but he couldn't place it. He caught a puzzled look on her face but walked on. A stage show with a live band and graphics projected onto a backcloth could work, he thought. It would be like a concept album on tour. Was the world ready for the return of the concept album? Did he just imagine it, or had he seen an advert for a tour of Jeff Wayne's *War of the Worlds*, including the voice of a long dead Richard Burton? He would check it out later.

***

Kate was chatting to one of her regulars as Rob passed the front of the salon. She recognised him when they made eye contact but took a second to work out where from. She could tell that he also recognised her, but then he was gone. She guessed correctly that he couldn't quite make the connection.

"Someone you know?" asked her customer.

"Kind of. Do you remember the band, West Coast Delta?"

"Remember them, I almost had one of their songs as the first dance at my wedding. Do you know 'Drunken Love'?"

"Yeah."

"The band we had were rotten. They couldn't do it. Do you know what we ended up with?"

"'Lady in Red' by Chris De Burgh?" said Kate sarcastically.

"God no. 'Every Step You Take', by the Police. I only found out afterwards that it was about a stalker. So, it ended up being kind of fitting."

"How has it been lately?"

"He's not been near me since the court case. The divorce is next month, so all's well that ends well," she laughed.

"Anyway," said Kate. "That was Rob, the singer from the Deltas."

"Who?"

"The guy who just passed by."

"Oh, right. I thought he was dead."

"No, that was Keith."

"So, do you know them?"

"I've met Rob. None of the others."

"Did you get his autograph?"

"No, it didn't seem appropriate at the time."

"That was a wasted opportunity."

"I suppose it was."

"Do you know what he said at the court case?" she said, moving back onto her ex. "He said that I assaulted him."

Kate carried on styling and nodding appropriately at each twist in the tale of the disastrous marriage, while remembering her last meeting with Rob.

They were both sixteen and Kate was going out with his cousin, Hugh. Rob lived in Hamilton but had been a frequent visitor to Pitside, staying for weekend. That night, a crowd of them went to the under-18 disco in the community centre. Hugh had got a bottle of some fortified wine, Eldorado if she remembered correctly. Just before they entered the community centre, Hugh had downed the bottle in one go. He then quickly made his way inside, past the youth workers before the effects took hold. They found a seat and Rob then asked Kate to dance. If anyone else had asked her, she would have assumed that they were chatting her up, but Rob was different. If he liked a song, he just wanted to dance to it. Kate even remembered the song. It was Japan's cover version of 'I Second That Emotion'.

Just as the song ended, Kate spotted Hugh coming towards them. The wine had kicked in and he did a sideways shuffle, one step forward, two to the side. He asked Kate if she wanted to dance. Hugh only ever danced when drunk. He then suddenly leaned over, stared at the floor and threw up. Kate jumped back to avoid the spray of Eldorado and bile. One of the youth workers was over beside them in a flash, telling Kate and Rob to get Hugh out of the disco. They each took an arm and guided him towards the door. Everyone watched and laughed. A few people cheered. Hugh looked up and proclaimed, "See her, I've shagged her." Another cheer went up from the watching crowd. The caretaker growled at them as he passed with a bucket of sawdust.

It was too early to go home, and they decided they better sober him first. They walked down to the headless virgin and sat him against a wall to sleep for an hour.

"He hasn't shagged me," said Kate.

"It's no-one's business if he has, I mean if you have … well you know what I mean."

"Yeah, but the whole village will think I have, and I haven't."

"You're sixteen, Kate. You'll be out of here soon anyway."

"Will I?"

"Well I will," said Rob. "I'm out of Hamilton next year. I'm going to start a band and I'm going to see the world."

And he did. He never came back to Pitside as far as Kate knew, and ten years later she saw him on TV. Twenty-six was old to have your first hit, but it didn't stop him, and he had, no doubt, seen the world too. Kate had dumped Hugh the next morning, but everyone in the village heard that Hugh, 'Shug' to all his friends, had shagged Kate. 'Shug' became 'Shagger' and to this day he was still named after an event that had not actually taken place.

***

Hugh was thinking about his problem with Jaffa. He had just one week to raise a thousand pounds. He could always just leave Pitside and never come back. That would be no great tragedy. But where would he go? What would he do? No matter how many times he asked himself the question he had no answers. Hugh's attention drifted back to the tutor. He stood there waving his arms about as he talked about the next exercise. Hugh had never seen anyone so animated without the use of alcohol. To make matters worse he kept looking at Hugh since he'd been stupid enough to volunteer a comment earlier on. No doubt he now saw Hugh an ally in his quest to turn the people of Pitside into hard-working citizens.

"So, that's the basic idea," said Gordon. "I want you to split back up into the same groups and have a chat about things you would do, perhaps things that you already do, for no money. Things which interest you or that capture your imagination."

The groups shuffled into the corners of the room and stared at each other, waiting for someone to break the silence.

"Right," said Hugh to his group. "We're here all day, so we might as well get on with it."

Silence from the others.

"I'll start then. I would eat, drink and have sex without anyone having to pay me to do it."

"I don't think that's the kind of thing he had in mind," said Sarah.

"I would go fishing," said one of the others. "I just love standing on a riverbank in total silence, away from everyone."

"Good," said Hugh. "Sarah, you write that up on the flipchart. Fishing."

"Why should I do the writing?"

"Because you're a neater writer than us and it means you don't have to give the feedback."

Sarah stood up and began writing.

"What about the drinking and sex?" she asked.

"We'll come back to that. What about you, John?"

"I'd make those little machines that they use on Robot Wars. I did one from a kit with my nephew and it was good fun. I wouldn't mind doing one from scratch."

"Okay. Write that up Sarah. Making Robots. Now what about you?"

"I don't really know."

"Come on, what do you do that you don't get paid for?"

"Cooking and cleaning," she joked.

"And do you enjoy it?"

"No, well apart from baking. I do enjoy that. I made my sister's wedding cake. Three tiers."

"Okay, write it up. Making wedding cakes."

"What about you, Shagger?"

"Like I said, drinking."

"If we've got to put something sensible up, so have you. What have you done lately?"

"Well, I did organise a night at the social club for nothing. In fact, it cost me money. Are any of you going to the night next week?"

"The last one wasn't very good."

"I've got a Karaoke this time."

"Really," said Sarah.

"Well maybe. I'm still trying to get it organised."

Sarah wrote up on the flipchart 'Organising Events'.

"I didn't say I enjoyed it, Sarah. I just said I did it without getting paid."

"But you do enjoy organising things. You took charge of this exercise, you're on the social club committee. You can't help yourself. You always want to be the person in charge."

Hugh realised it was true. He had just become so depressed over the debt he owed to Jaffa that he had lost sight of the enjoyment he used to get from it.

"Listen. What would make you come to the fundraiser next week? What would make it worth going to?"

"Is this part of the exercise?" asked Sarah.

"No, but none of the other groups have written a thing up yet and we're finished. So, come on. What would make you come next week?"

"Do you want me to write it up on the flipchart?" asked Sarah.

"Yes, but start a new page. We don't want to upset George."

"It's Gordon," said Sarah.

"Karaoke write that up. Now, what else?" asked Hugh.

"Food, drink and sex."

***

Hugh left the course for lunch in a surprisingly good mood. The last few days had been a dark time. He realised that he had lost sight of his own abilities. Hugh had been invited onto the social club committee because people recognised his talent for organisation. Admittedly they were short of volunteers but all the same, they still asked him. It had been Hugh's idea to create the free drink allocation for committee meetings and he had introduced other innovations. The first few nights he had organised had been a great success, which was what had attracted Jaffa's attention. If Hugh could just get Jaffa out of his hair, things would get back to normal. The folk on the course had come up with some suggestions for the night. Nothing spectacular, but worth doing. The Karaoke was the top of the list. People always loved that after a few drinks. Hugh would organise a best male singer and best female singer prize. He could get Armando to put up a couple of fish suppers as prizes. Jaffa could give them some DVDs. Three or four movies that weren't in the cinema yet. They could do a coin throw for them. Pound a go, the coin nearest the DVDs wins them. The club also had some beer which was almost out of date. They had bought in a few crates of imported bottled beer which hadn't taken off. *Bier of Limburg* tasted rough, but it was 5% alcohol. They would have to write it off in a couple of weeks anyway, so they would be happy to give it away for a raffle. There were ninety-six bottles just gathering dust in the storeroom. They could get a couple of cigarette cartons from Jaffa as well. They should be able to charge two quid for a raffle ticket with almost a hundred beers and 400 cigarettes up for grabs. If they could get about 150 people through the door on the night and the coin throw and raffle tickets did well, they could clear £1000 after costs. Jaffa was right. It could be done. The key was the Karaoke. That was what would get people through the door in the first place. Hugh felt his life being reclaimed.

"Roll and chips, Armando."

"I can't tempt you with anything else?"

"No thanks. Listen, we're having a fundraiser next week. How do you fancy putting up a couple of gift vouchers for the Karaoke prize?"

"Who's the money for?"

"Well, you know."

"Shagger, I can't support them. You know that."

"What if I pay for them?"

"Well, I can't stop you buying something from me."

"How about half price?"

"You should be in business. Okay, half price."

Hugh delved into his pocket to pay for the chip roll.

"Forget it. This one's on me," said Armando. "Just don't tell anyone."

Hugh went next door into the shop.

"No luck," said Davy.

"The Karaoke?" asked Hugh.

Davy nodded. "He's booked up for the next six weeks."

"Shit. Does he know anyone else that could do it?"

"Afraid not. He said he'll do it if he gets a cancellation, but that's unlikely."

Hugh left the shop and threw his roll in the bin. His appetite was gone. He'd left it too late to turn things around. Hugh headed back to the community centre. That was it, he was finished. He would just have to face the fact that the night was going to be a washout and he would get a beating at the end of it. Probably the best thing he could do was to get drunk and stay drunk in the hope that it would dull the pain. Plan B wasn't great, but it was all he had.

***

The Halycon was dreamt up as a private member's club for Glasgow's media movers and shakers. The only problem being that Glasgow didn't have enough media movers and shakers to make the place viable, even if all of them joined. The club, therefore, quickly adapted to become the meeting place for Glasgow's creative industries. In practice that meant anyone who wasn't a footballer or a gangster, these two groups already being catered for in most other clubs in town. Rob arrived early and sat in the reading room with a whisky and a coffee, flicking through Orpheus Jones. The reading room was a modern take on a gentleman's club. Leather armchairs and occasional tables with patterned wallpaper. Look closely though and the repeating pattern on the walls was a mother pushing a pram past a tower block. The pictures hanging on the wall were blank canvases combined with gilt frames.

"Can I get you anything else, sir?" asked the waitress in the regulation black wrap dress over black trousers.

"Another whisky thanks."

"Another Laphroaig or would you care to try our 18-year-old Bunnahabhain?"

"Laphroaig is fine. Once you've had one, your palette is ruined for any other whisky, don't you think?"

"Unless it's another Islay malt."

"Okay, I'll take the Bunnahabhain."

"Very good, sir. I will bring your guests through when they arrive."

"Tell me," asked Rob. "Is the Bunnahabhain more expensive?"

"Yes, it is, sir. That's why I recommended it, but you will enjoy it."

Rob smiled. Even the deference of the staff was knowingly ironic.

Lisa and her agent, Brian, arrived together. They were shown through to the reading room. She shook her head when she saw Rob. He was slumped in the chair, his face obscured by another comic book.

"Rob," she said loudly, hoping he would put it down before Brian noticed.

Rob lowered the book without putting it down. "Hi Lisa. Got here a little early."

"Interesting reading," said Brian.

"It is," said Rob, putting the book down at last.

"So, shall we go through for lunch?" Lisa changed the subject.

"They do an afternoon tea," said Rob. "We could just stay here and have that. It's more comfortable than the restaurant."

"Fine, whatever." Even when Rob was out somewhere nice, he slouched in his chair.

Eating their lunch, they discussed the previous night's program.

"Travel TV has good real estate," said Brian. "Four five six."

"I don't follow," said Rob.

"Think about it. Four five six. They're right next to each other. Easy to remember. The channel number does count in a multi-channel environment, and four five six is a good number."

"So, they get good viewing figures then?"

"For the market position yes, absolutely."

"What kind of figures are you talking about?"

"Well let's not get into demographics over lunch," said Brian. "But they're good. It will help Lisa."

"Brian was telling me on the way over, Rob, it's D-Day next week for *Doghouse Makeover*."

"That's good, Lisa. It's been quite stressful waiting to hear. It will be good to know one way or another."

"This would be a real step-change in Lisa's career." Turning to her Brain said, "You would then be in a space where you can start to develop the human brand."

"The human brand?" Rob screwed up his eyes.

"The person as the brand. Do you realise how big, for example, the pet food business is? It's huge. Check out the supermarket the next time you're in. They typically have a whole aisle given over to pet food. If you have a human brand that you can align to that industry, the potential is huge."

"What do you mean? Lisa Ward dog food?"

"Hey, look at Paul Newman salad dressing. That's a multi-million-pound industry."

"I know," said Rob. "But dog food?"

"Brian is just using that as an example, Rob. It could be anything. It could be furnishings or fabric freshener or pet insurance."

"The endorsement industry is huge," said Brian. "You are a human brand, Rob. Whether you like the name or not doesn't matter. That's what you are. And you could exploit it if you wanted."

"Right, well that's something I wouldn't want to rush into."

"I know," said Lisa. "Anyway, listen to us talking as if I've already been offered the job. Talk about counting your chickens."

***

Gordon looked at his watch. It was three o'clock. If he could get packed up and out of Pitside by four, he would be back in town by five. It had been a long day, but not as bad as he had first expected.

"Right, how about we do one more exercise and then we call it a day. We are scheduled to finish at four thirty, but if we can aim for half three, I'm happy to finish early. Is that okay with you?"

For the first time that day he got a positive response from everybody. People sat up and smiled, or at least paid attention.

"Let's finish off on a high. So, has anyone heard of Kevin Bacon?"

"The actor?" said Sarah.

"Yes," said Gordon. "Now, can anyone name a film he's been in?"

"*Dirty Dancing*."

"No," said Gordon. "That was Patrick Swayze"

"Are you sure?"

"Yes."

"No," someone else said. "Kevin Bacon was definitely in *Dirty Dancing*."

"No, he wasn't," said Gordon. "You are possibly thinking of *Footloose*. Can anyone name any other movies he's been in?"

"I thought he was in *Dirty Dancing* too," said another course member.

"Well he wasn't, so let's move on folks. Another movie?"

"*Saving Private Ryan*?"

"No," said Gordon.

"*Apocalypse Now*?"

"No."

"*Deliverance*?"

"Nope."

"*Deer Hunter*?"

"Look," said Gordon, exasperated. "Don't guess. This isn't the exercise. This is just an introduction to it. Don't guess. If you don't know, don't guess, alright."

"*Ghost*," someone said.

"Jesus, that was Patrick Swayze as well."

"*Titanic*?"

"Right stop. The point I was trying to make is that Kevin Bacon has been in a lot of movies. Can we just accept that premise?"

"But he wasn't in any of the ones we came up with?"

"No, but he has been in a lot of movies," said Gordon.

"*Star Wars*," someone shouted.

Gordon felt the anger rising but noticed some of course participants fighting to contain their laughter. With the end of the day in sight they were now baiting him. He took a breath, determined not to give in to the provocation.

"Forget Kevin Bacon," he said. "Has anyone heard of the six degrees of separation?"

"Was he in that too?"

The group was now struggling, avoiding eye contact with each other, shoulders twitching. Gordon just had to fight past it.

"It is a theory that anyone can connect with anyone else in the world through no more than six people. For example, I happen to know my local MP. He knows the foreign secretary, who knows the prime minister who knows the U.S. president. Therefore, I can connect to the president through three people. What I want you all to do is write your name in the centre of a blank sheet of paper. Have three or four lines coming out from your name and write the name of someone you know personally at the other end of each line. Then do the same for each of the names. Three or four lines coming out from them. Write the names of three or four people they know. Preferably someone you don't know personally. Then keep repeating this up to six times, so that you are at the centre of six layers of people. Now, I know that you might only manage one or two layers to start with, but this will be your homework for next week. I want you to contact some of the people on your list and find out who they know. Ask them to do the same and see if you can get to six layers. You might find it useful to do it using a theme. For example, you might try and make a connection to a certain profession or you might try and make a connection to someone in Australia or Canada. The point of this exercise is to help you realise how many connections you have that you could use in your attempt to find a job or achieve anything else for that matter. I know it's a lot to take in, but is that clear?"

"What does Kevin Bacon have to do with it? Have we to try and connect to him?"

"So, just make a start," said Gordon. "I will come around and talk through the exercise one to one if anyone's not clear. If it runs on beyond half three, that's okay. As I said, we are due to finish at half four. Half three, half four, either suits me."

They all went quiet and began to work at the threat of an extra hour. Hugh wrote his name down in the centre of the page. He then wrote a few names round his. His mother, Kenny, a few others. He then paused and thought of a theme. Who's got a grand to spare, he thought. Who's got a grand to spare? Hugh looked at his mother's name. She didn't. None of the family did. Then it struck him. Family. Hugh picked up his pen and wrote another name on the paper. Rob.

*\*\*\**

Rob made his way home from lunch, retracing his route up Gibson Street. Remembering the woman in the hair salon he slowed his pace as he approached it. He had thought about her after lunch but still couldn't place her. He looked into the shop but couldn't see her. Rob pulled a flyer for a nightclub out of his pocket, using it as a reason to stop, and threw it in the bin. He looked again but still couldn't see her.

"You looking for a haircut?"

Rob turned to see her standing at the door. He was taken aback by this and stumbled over a response. "Eh, well …"

"Come on in," she said.

Rob followed her into the shop and handed her his jacket.

"You'll need a wash," she said. "I'll get you a coffee."

Rob took this as a statement rather than a question and so had his hair washed. By the time he found himself sitting in front of a mirror with a cup of coffee, he still hadn't managed to successfully dredge his memory.

"You obviously don't remember my name. It's Kate."

"Right. We have met, haven't we? I'm Rob."

"Yes, I know. So, what do you want done with your hair?"

"Well, I don't know. I'm going to a funeral tomorrow."

"We don't have a funeral haircut as such, but I could just tidy it up?"

"Okay."

Kate began to work.

"I'm sorry but I just can't remember where we have met. Give me a clue."

"A clue. Mmh, Japan. I second that emotion."

"It was a figure of speech. Where did we meet?"

"Just go with the clue."

Rob closed his eyes and thought. Nothing came. "I do like the song. Not sure the Japan version is my favourite though. You know it's actually a Smokey Robinson number?"

"Really. Next you'll be telling me that Sid Vicious didn't write My Way."

"I sang it live on TV once. Were you part of the make-up team?"

Kate laughed. "No, try again."

Rob had a few more goes and then gave up. After twenty minutes of small talk, Kate finished.

"That will do for the funeral," she said. "Personally, I think you could do with most of it off but have a think about it and come back if you want me to finish it."

"So, come on, where do I know you from?"

"If you haven't remembered by the time you come back, I'll tell you then. That's the best I can do."

"Is that how you drum up business?"

"It all helps."

"So, I guess I'll be back then."

"I guess so."

After Rob left, Kate wondered to herself why she hadn't just told him. It was fun having him guess, but that wasn't it. What would she have said? I used to go out with that no-hope loser of a cousin of yours. It just wasn't something she wanted to remind herself or anyone else of. I knew your cousin. She could say that if he came back. I used to hang out with your cousin. That would do. Why was it that teenage memories stayed so strong? Only teenage memories could make Kate blush. Anything that had happened since, she could laugh off as stupidity. Anything that happened before her teenage years were just part of childhood. Teenage memories, they burned like no others, never to be forgotten, always defining the person, no matter how much had been done or achieved since. Shagger's ex, that was what she was still known as in Pitside. He'd had several girlfriends since Kate and had even lived with one of them for a few years, but Kate was and always would be Shagger's ex.

***

"He just doesn't take my career seriously," said Lisa.

Scott, sitting opposite her in the canteen, nodded enthusiastically.

"He just couldn't take the whole co-branding thing seriously, but he has his songs in adverts."

"I know. Sometimes success breeds a kind of … I don't know, a kind of …"

"Arrogance."

Scott sighed as if Lisa had forced it out of him. "That's not the word I would have used but yes."

"You know, he never actually does anything these days. When we met him in the Halcyon, he was reading a comic. Reading a comic," she repeated.

Scott shook his head.

"Has he just lost it? Is that the problem?"

"You know that most of the Delta's songs were credited jointly to Rob and Keith?"

Lisa nodded.

Scott shook his head. "That was an agreement they came to early on when they did write together. Someone would come up with a melody and a chorus, the other would finish it off. Towards the end that isn't how it worked. It was mostly Keith."

He had her hook line and sinker. She stared intently at Scott, expecting more. "Why do you think the band broke up after Keith died? Meanwhile Rob sits back and collects half the royalties."

Lisa shook her head. "It makes so much sense," she said.

Scott was amazed at himself. He was making this up as he spoke, but it sounded completely authentic. What the hell, Rob was never going to get the band back together. He had nothing to lose.

# Chapter 3

She really is stunning, thought Rob, as he watched Lisa dry her hair. He lay in bed as she sat at the dressing table moving her head from side to side running her hands through her long blonde hair. She had been out for a morning run, showered and was now preparing herself for the day ahead. Rob wanted to drag her back to bed and make love to her. This surprised him as it had been so long. How had he forgotten how great she looked? Probably because he went to bed after she was asleep every night and got up after she left for work every morning. Sitting there in her underwear, unselfconscious, she was beautiful. They never seemed to spend any real time together and that was probably his fault. The hairdryer clicked off and Lisa picked up the straighteners.

"It's good of you come to the funeral today," said Rob.

"We are a couple."

"It hasn't felt like it lately, has it?"

"Everyone goes through bad patches."

Rob was about to clarify whether she meant the relationship was going through a bad patch or he was going through one, but he let it pass. Things had been so bad between them that any respite from the bitterness was welcome.

"Why don't you come back to bed? We've plenty of time."

"Does the thought of funerals turn you on?"

"No, but that underwear does."

"Once I've started with the straighteners, there's no way I'm going to mess my hair up. You should know that by now."

"Maybe later?"

"After a day with the grieving family? Sure, that does it for me too."

Rob drove as they set off to pick up his father. As they headed out of the city Lisa stared out the window at the road signs declaring 'SOUTH'. That was where she was headed. Within a couple of days, she would know what was happening with the program and she would be off. Looking over at Rob, she wondered why he had stayed in Scotland after he had made it with the band. Despite Scott's claims that Rob hadn't written the band's songs, he had still been the lead singer. He had toured the world, yet here he was, still stuck in Glasgow.

"Why did you never leave?" she asked.

"What do you mean?"

"Glasgow, Scotland. Why didn't you leave after you made it?"

"The world's a smaller place than it used to be," he said. "It never stopped us doing anything we wanted to do. Fans don't care about where you live. They just like your music, or they don't."

"But aren't there other places you'd rather be?"

Rob took the cut-off for Hamilton.

"There were places other than Hamilton I wanted to be," he said.

"What about Glasgow?"

"Sometimes there are places I'd rather be than Glasgow. When there are, I go and then I come back. I even have a name for it. I call it holidays."

"Funny"

"You know what, any city with a couple of hundred thousand people and a university has plenty going on if you take the trouble to look and if you make stuff it doesn't matter where you are. If you're a critic or a presenter, it does."

"Like me?"

"Yeah, of course. That's why you're asking isn't it? You're wondering whether you should be based in London for the sake of your career."

Lisa was taken aback. "Well, it is something I have been thinking about, yes. Is it that obvious?"

"This new job is all you've talked about for weeks, then you ask me why I stayed in Glasgow, so yeah it is pretty obvious. Anyway, if I hadn't stayed you wouldn't have met me and it's not all been bad has it?"

Lisa smiled. "No, no it hasn't. And what if I do get the job?"

"Then I guess we'll need to decide," said Rob as he brought the car to a stop outside his father's house.

His father came out of the house immediately, already with his overcoat on. He made a show of checking his watch and then locked the door behind him.

"Guess he's been ready for a while," said Rob

"Rob, Lisa," said his father as he climbed into the back of the car.

"I'm not late, am I?"

"No, but I thought you might get here a little early. How are you, Lisa?"

"Fine, how are you holding up, Bert?"

"Never really liked him to be honest, but he was Ann's brother, and it's another link with her gone." Tears welled up in his eyes.

Lisa passed over a tissue.

"Thanks, Lisa, come on, Rob, let's get going."

Rob shook his head but said nothing. His father was a master at using the memory of Rob's mother to control situations.

"Don't want to be late," said Bert. "It's very disrespectful."

"We'll be there in plenty of time."

Lisa wanted to ask Rob what he had meant when he said, "we'll need to decide." Did he mean 'we' need to decide whether to move, or did he mean 'we' need to decide whether to stay together? If both were an option what did she want? Rob was not the love of her life, she knew that much. Would Rob try and come with her if she moved to London? That wasn't really in the plan.

*** 

Hugh woke up on the couch with the sound of the door being knocked. He pulled the duvet round him and shuffled through to the hall.

"Are you not ready yet?" said his mother, when he opened the door.

"Come on in. I'll be five minutes."

"The taxi's due in five minutes."

"Well that's fine because I'll be ready in five minutes. Make me a tea, will you?"

"This is a funeral, you know. We can't be late."

"Right. Five minutes, tea, please."

Hugh went upstairs to the bathroom and splashed cold water on his face. His head ached from the night before. He soaked a hand towel, wrung the water out and wrapped it round his head. The coolness felt good and relieved some of the pain. As he got dressed Hugh discarded the belt that went with his black trousers. It was still stretched and misshapen from the attempted hanging. He put on the eagle motif belt, thinking it looked smarter. He then grabbed his white shirt, a zipper top and headed downstairs.

"I couldn't find a single clean cup," his mother said, handing him a tea.

"I just wash them as I need them. Works fine for me."

"Take the towel off your head."

"Right." Hugh threw the towel onto a chair.

"Don't leave it there it will make your chair damp."

"Will we wait outside for the taxi? You might find it a little less upsetting if you're not looking around my house."

"You're not moving back in with me."

"Who asked?" said Hugh as he finished dressing. "Why would I want to?"

"You don't know how to look after yourself, do you?"

"I'm fine. Just had a few drinks last night, that's all. I know you've got your own life, Mum. You don't want me there cramping your style when you bring guys back from the singles club."

"It's not a singles club, it's a friendship society."

"Is that what they call it these days?"

"There's the taxi, come on let's go."

Hugh got into the front of the taxi, still drinking his tea.

"If you spill that, I'll charge you an extra fiver," said the driver.

"Fine thanks, Jim. Rigburn cemetery."

"Do you want me to wait when we get there?"

"No," said Hugh's mother. "We should be able to get a lift off someone."

Hugh took sips of his tea, covering the top of the cup with his hand between drinks. The road twisted and turned, and Hugh began to feel a rumbling in his stomach. He shut his eyes and began to breathe slowly and deeply.

"Do you need me to stop, Shagger?" asked the driver.

Hugh shook his head and mumbled.

"If you're sick, it'll cost you the price of a full valet."

"What were you drinking last night anyway?" asked his mother.

"Please," mumbled Hugh. "Let me be."

Hugh had forgotten how bad the roads were between the villages, but if everyone left him alone, he would make it. He drifted into a dreamlike state, every movement feeling exaggerated and in slow motion. Now, he thought. Right now, I could take anything that Jaffa would do to me. His body felt out of sync, disconnected.

"Here we are," said the taxi driver, stopping the car at last.

Hugh opened the door and got out. He sat down on the ground, hung his head between his knees and tried not to move.

Hugh's mother paid the taxi driver and got out of the car. Standing over him she said, "Just as well we're early and no one can see you like this."

"We're early?" said Hugh looking up at her.

"Come on, you can't sit there. You'll block the road."

"I need to sit down."

"Go and find a quiet spot and stay out of sight until you feel better."

Hugh stood up and began to walk slowly into the graveyard.

"You forgot this," said his mother handing him the empty mug.

"Thanks."

"And sort your tie."

***

After leaving Hamilton, Rob re-joined the motorway and followed the signs south. After about ten miles he took the Rigburn turn-off and headed up the hill to the cemetery which overlooked the motorway. A few people had already arrived and were waiting at the entrance. Rob parked the car and they got out. The hearse arrived as they were talking to relatives and everyone followed the car into the cemetery and made their way to the graveside.

Standing there, Lisa's thoughts began to drift. The minister was conducting the service, but she found it hard to hear him over the noise of traffic from the road below. Looking into the distance she saw a figure standing up from behind a gravestone. He looked over towards the funeral and began to make his way over. He was dressed in black, so presumably he was here for the funeral, but he also seemed to be carrying a cup. As he got closer, he stuffed it into the pocket of his zipper top. Lisa looked around. No one else seemed to have noticed him, or if they did, they didn't seem to find it strange. As he got closer, he seemed to smile at her and headed in her direction. Lisa pulled closer to Rob.

"Rob, how's it going?" he said loudly.

Rob said something but it was drowned out by a passing lorry.

"What's that," shouted Hugh, cupping his ear.

Rob put a finger to his lips and then pointed to the minister.

"Oh, right."

***

"So, how are you Rob," asked Hugh as they walked back towards the car park.

"Good. Lisa, this is my cousin, Hugh."

"Nice to meet you."

"Are you two married or what?"

"No, not married."

"Listen, have you got space for two? Mum and I are looking for a lift down to the lodge. You are going, back aren't you?"

"Yeah, that should be fine."

"I'll go and find Mum. See you in a minute."

Rob, Lisa and his father waited in the car, while Hugh looked for his mother amongst the mourners.

"So, this guy Hugh," said Lisa.

"Complete numpty," said Rob's father.

"How exactly is he related to you?"

"Through Rob's mum," said Bert. "Nothing to do with my side of the family."

"He's not that bad. We had some great times together as kids."

"Nice wheels," said Hugh, opening the door for his mother.

"Thanks. Must be about five years since I last saw you, Hugh. You came to a concert in Glasgow."

"Weddings and funerals eh? Maybe you two should get hitched. Good excuse for a party."

Rob let the comment pass without reply.

After a couple of minutes Hugh leaned forward, "You'll need to stop the car."

"What?"

"You'll need to stop, now."

"He was almost sick on the way here," said Hugh's mother.

Rob pulled the car over onto the grass verge and Hugh quickly got out. He took a couple of steps forward and then threw up. Lisa watched out of the window as he spat out a final long string of bile and phlegm, then wiped his mouth. Hugh looked over at her and smiled.

"I thought I recognised you," said Hugh, getting back into the car. "You're on TV, aren't you?"

"Yes."

"Weather?"

"I'm not the weather girl. I'm the lunchtime entertainment anchor."

"Anchor?" said Hugh. "You do look like that weather girl. The two of you could be sisters."

"Well, thanks I guess."

"Imagine that. Rob going out with a TV star. What's your name again?"

"Lisa, Lisa Ward."

"Got you. So, has he never proposed to you, Lisa?"

***

"I'm happy to drive if you want to have a drink," said Lisa.

"No, I need to keep an eye on my dad. He can get a bit out of hand at these things. You go ahead and get one."

"How long do we need to stay for?"

"A few hours, maximum."

"Okay, I'll have a wine."

Rob shouted over the crowd gathered round the bar to Hugh who was getting a round in. He then took Lisa's coat and went to find the cloakroom. Lisa stood alone feeling slightly awkward.

Hugh appeared with the drinks and handed Lisa a wine.

"Thank you." As she took a drink Lisa couldn't help noticing that Hugh was staring at her breasts.

Looking up from her cleavage, Hugh's gaze met Lisa's. "So," he said. "You're a Catholic then?"

"Sorry?"

"You're a Catholic," he repeated, nodding at her breasts. "The crucifix," he said by way of an explanation.

Lisa touched her cross." Is that a problem?"

"No, no problem, I'm just saying. It's funny how they have that little Jesus on it though isn't it?"

"They?"

"Just seems a bit, I don't know. A bit over the top."

"Right. And are you religious, Hugh?"

"No, I'm a Protestant." he said smiling.

"Well, I guess it would seem over the top then."

Rob reappeared. "Will we grab a seat?" he said.

"Let's."

"Listen Rob," said Hugh. "We should keep in touch. Give me your address and we can go out for a drink sometime."

"Sure. We can swap details later."

***

Hugh borrowed a pen and a beer mat from the bar and headed over to the table where Rob was sitting. He had decided that it would be wise to get Rob's details just in case they didn't get a chance to talk in private. Hugh didn't fancy bringing up the topic of a loan with Rob's girlfriend listening. The crucifix was the first thing he thought of when she caught him staring at her fantastic cleavage, but she had obviously taken offence.

"Here you go, Rob," he said handing him the pen and beer mat.

"Right." Rob wrote his address and phone number down.

"Are you an ornithologist, Hugh?" asked Lisa.

"No, why?"

"Oh nothing, it's just that eagle belt buckle. I thought it might mean something. A bit over the top for a funeral though. Don't you think?"

"The other one is all stretched."

"The other one. You mean there's two?"

"Excuse me," interrupted a waitress putting down a plate of food on the table.

"Better find a seat," said Hugh. "I'll catch you later."

"What was that about?" asked Rob.

"Nothing."

The minister stood up and rapped his knuckles on the table to get silence.

"Lord, we thank you for the bounty you have placed before us. We give thanks too for the support of friends and relatives, present and absent. Amid the riches you have laid before us, we recognise that life is not all steak pie and chips. What you give, you also take away. We may not always understand, Lord, but we accept the wisdom of all that you do. May your presence be amongst us. Amen."

"I don't think I've ever heard steak pie and chips mentioned in a prayer before," said Lisa.

"No ordinary pies," said Rob's father. "These are from Campbell Sutherland, the butcher. He's won gold medals with his pies."

"I'm not making fun of the meal. It just seems strange in a prayer."

"I thought he killed some customers a few years ago?" said Rob.

"He did," said his father. "E-coli, but that was the cold meat. If you cook his stuff it's fine. Just make sure the pie's piping hot in the middle."

"Eat up, Lisa."

Lisa looked down at the pie on her plate. "I'm not that hungry."

\*\*\*

"Thanks for coming," said Raymond.

"Not at all," said Rob. "I didn't know your dad had been so ill."

"He left it too late to go to the doctor. You know what they can be like. By the time he had been diagnosed it had spread too far."

"Did he suffer much at the end?" asked Rob's father.

"I'd like to say no, but yes it was tough."

"It must be hard," said Rob.

"Well, it's not how I planned to spend my birthday, that's for sure."

"It's your birthday today?"

"Yes."

"Alright, Raymondo?" said Hugh, joining the group.

"Hello Hugh. Listen, I better go and mingle." Raymond wandered off to talk to another group.

"Raymondo?" said Bert. "It's his dad's funeral and you come breezing up calling him Raymondo?"

"Hmm, you're right, Uncle Bert. I'll apologise to him later. Listen, can I have a quiet word with Rob?"

"With pleasure. I need a drink."

"Dad, slow down a bit, will you?" said Rob as his father headed for the bar.

"Rob," said Hugh in his serious voice.

"What?"

"I need your help. I'm in a bit of trouble."

"Well, if I can help I will. What's the problem?"

"The thing is, I need some money and I need it pretty quickly. In fact, within the next couple of days."

"Right. So, it's money?"

"I would pay it back, no question. It's just that the guy I owe it to …"

"No."

"What do you mean no?"

"No. All you're doing is moving debt around. You're not solving anything. Instead of owing one person money, you'll owe me. If you ever pay me off it will be by borrowing it off someone else."

"Come on, Rob, you can afford it."

"Probably, but the answer's no. If you were looking for me to help you help yourself then fine, but you're not. You're just looking to get bailed out until the next time."

"That's good isn't it? You can save the planet, but you won't help a relative?"

"I'm not trying to save the planet either, Hugh. I don't know where you got that idea."

"Pop stars, all the same. Just forget it," he said storming off.

Forgotten already, thought Rob. The last time he'd seen Hugh was backstage at a concert in Glasgow for which Rob had sent him two guest passes. Hugh and his friend had stolen a couple of bottles of spirits from the hospitality suite and borrowed money for a taxi home. It was only when Hugh had asked for money that Rob had remembered. The guy saw him as more of an opportunity than a relative.

***

"And do you ever regret it?" Lisa asked Raymond's wife.

"Moving to London? No. There were more opportunities for us down there and for the kids too. I hated Rigburn. All the petty bigotry. Did you notice the park fence is painted blue?"

"No."

"Years ago, the council painted it green, just like park fences everywhere. But oh no, the locals wouldn't have it. Green is a Catholic colour, an Irish colour. There was such an outcry that the council had to come back and paint it blue again. And do you know what? They think that's progress. The railings used to be one red, one white, one blue, all the way round the park."

"Rob's cousin, Hugh, pointed out to me that I'm a Catholic."

"Moron."

"Ladies and gentlemen, can I have your attention," shouted Rob's father.

The noise of people talking subsided as Bert rapped the table a few times with the base of his whisky tumbler.

"Thank you. Not many of you might know this, but today is Raymond's birthday. Now we all know he isn't going to feel like celebrating, but I thought that it would be wrong for it to go unmarked. So, a toast to Raymond," Bert lifted his glass high. "Raymond, you've given your dad a good send off and if he were here, he would say thank you and happy birthday, happy birthday."

Every joined in and raised a glass. Raymond smiled and nodded in thanks to Rob's father.

Bert then began to sing. He sung in a slow, sad, ironic lament.

> Happy ... birthday ... to ... you
>
> Happy ... birthday ... to ... you

He then swung his arm up into the air in a bid to get everyone to join in.

> Happy ... birthday ... dear ... Raymond

Despite the encouragement, Bert was still on his own. Rob tried not to catch anyone's eye as the guests looked around at each other in astonishment.

> Happy... birthday ... to ... you

Rob scanned the room for Lisa. She was sitting next to Raymond's wife and looking like she wanted the ground to swallow her up.

"Rob," said Hugh, tapping him on the elbow. "I really do need the money. Let me explain."

"Fuck off Hugh," said Rob, pushing past him to rescue Lisa from her embarrassment.

\*\*\*

"I don't think he was offended," said Lisa, as they drove back into town after dropping Rob's father off.

"Raymond's a nice guy and he would never admit it."

"Your dad did mean well."

"I suppose."

Lisa decided to leave Rob to his thoughts and stared out of the window.

"Did you hear him going on about Chinese funerals, how they wear white and it's a celebration?"

"He was just trying to justify himself," said Lisa. "Do you think it's true? I can't imagine anyone really celebrating at a funeral of someone they loved, can you?"

"Who knows? That's just his thing. Little known facts from around the world. I think he gets them all from the Readers Digest."

"Did you know that the park railings in Rigburn are blue?" said Lisa.

"God, you're starting to sound like him now."

"No, but apparently they are. Everyone objected to them being green. Raymond's wife told me."

"There's probably a Chinese version of my dad telling people about that and the traffic lights."

"Traffic lights?"

"She didn't tell you about the traffic lights? They have a metal grid over the green filter to stop it being vandalised."

"No?"

"Yeah. There's one set of traffic lights in Rigburn and the green filter kept getting smashed or stolen. Someone replaced it with a piece of blue plastic one time."

"I'm going to London, Rob."

"I know."

"It's where the opportunities are."

"You're right."

Lisa sat back and closed her eyes. Does he think he's coming with me? she thought. His cousin Hugh looked a little like Rob. A deviant mutation from the foothills of Lanarkshire. Rob wasn't as bad as that, but he was probably turning back into Lanarkshire man, slowly but surely, sitting in the house every day reading comics and watching movies. If he really wanted to keep a career in music, he could have probably got a part in a musical. Everyone had appeared in *Chicago* over the last few years. At least Rob could sing. He could have been Billy Flynn in a touring production at the very least.

***

Rob switched off the music when he saw Lisa nodding off. He thought back to Hugh asking him for money and it still annoyed him. As much as he had enjoyed Hugh's company in the past, Rob had always ended up bailing him out in one way or another. Rob remembered the time Hugh got thrown out of the disco in the community centre after throwing up. Rob and Hugh's girlfriend had to take care of him until he was sober enough to go home.

Kate, he thought. That's who she was. Kate, Hugh's ex-girlfriend. The two of them danced to Japan's version of 'I Second That Emotion'. He held her in his arms as they danced. It was a much slower version than the Miracles' original and was really one for the couples. It wasn't a bad version remembered through the lens of that night. David Sylvian's voice conveyed both hope and regret. Hope that this was the woman he could spend the rest of his life with, and regret and sadness that she probably wasn't. Rob looked over at Lisa sleeping in the passenger seat and was struck, as he had been many times before, at how much truth and meaning could be conveyed in a simply constructed three-minute song.

## Chapter 4

Rob woke early on Sunday and left Lisa sleeping. He sat down at the kitchen table with his two new copies of Orpheus Jones and began to cut out each picture, spreading them out on the table as he did so. After he had cut out the first five or six pages, he then began to group the images into themes. He was sure he could do something with this. The first theme that was emerging was denial. Orpheus cannot believe that the love of his life was gone. Rob put the other pictures to one side and spread out the denial pictures. He nodded to himself. Several pictures showed Orpheus dreaming. In his dreams, his girlfriend, Izzi, was not dead. He had just forgotten about her. He came across her sitting in the living room of their flat and she asked him where he had been. He apologised for forgetting to visit her and held her hand. Rob knew this dream. He had experienced ones like this about his mother and about Keith. The settings were often different, but it was essentially the same dream. He had forgotten to visit people he knew who were dead. He had neglected them. Rob had never spoken of these dreams to anyone. Never given them that much thought. Now focusing on the images laid out before him, Rob realised that it was probably quite a common experience. This could be a song. A song of apology to the dead. 'I try not to forget you, but sometimes I do,' said the character on the page. 'If I could remember you better, you would still be here' he said in another frame. Rob recognised the sentiment.

Lisa appeared at the kitchen door, full of sleep. She walked over to the table and stared at the pictures spread out. Shaking her head, she turned and walked away.

"Is there a problem?" asked Rob.

"No," she mumbled. "I'm just going for a quick shower."

"I'll make some coffee."

Lisa lifted her face up into the spray of hot water. The noise and sensation blanked out her thoughts. That was what she needed. She needed a break from herself, constantly trying to work out whether she had got the job, whether she should feel angry at Rob or sorry for him. It had started on the way back from the funeral last night and it just would not stop. Too much thought. Lisa stepped out of the shower and dried herself, trying to slow down the flood of thoughts as she did so. What is he doing with all those comics?

"Coffee?"

"Thanks." Lisa sat down at the kitchen table. She picked up one of the pictures Rob had cut out. She looked it at and turned it over a few times. "What are you doing with all these comics, Rob? Every time I see you these days, you're reading one. Now you're cutting them up."

"It's the same one, Lisa. It's Orpheus Jones. I'm thinking of doing something with it."

"What can you possibly do with a comic?"

Rob handed Lisa a coffee and sat down. "Either a concept album or a stage show. I'm not sure yet."

Lisa shook her head. "Rob, please don't. People will think you've gone mad. Not a comic, please."

"It's a graphic novel."

Lisa suppressed a laugh. "Well sorry. Not being a connoisseur of these things, I find it hard to tell the difference between a comic and 'graphic novel'. Tell me, is Batman a comic or a graphic novel?"

"It can be both. The Frank Miller series *The Dark Knight Returns* started life as a comic, albeit in prestige format, but it was later produced as a graphic novel …"

"Okay, let's just leave it. All I'm saying is that you do still have a reputation, Rob. Think about it."

***

Scott had been distracted ever since he had spoken to Lisa on Friday afternoon. He didn't regret telling her that Rob hadn't written any of the later songs, but he was worried about it. On reflection, he still hoped that a reunion with the band was possible. If Rob found out what he had been saying, there would be no chance of that ever happening and Lisa would find out that it was a lie. How, he asked himself, had he got into the situation where he wanted something from both sides of the same relationship? What made it worse was that it was now beginning to affect his career.

Scott had spent the previous day watching Motherwell play Inverness Caley. It was excruciating. The game consisted of one side kicking the ball as far up the park as possible, opposing players heading the ball back and forward until someone else finally managed to get a foot to it and battered it back up the other end. Sitting in the stand he felt as though he was watching an oversized game of tennis, his head moving one way, then the other. At least he wasn't commentating on the thing. The only reason he had come to the match was because he had been invited by the new chief executive of the TV station. Fergus Veitch had been head-hunted from the Hong Kong office of the media consultancy Booth, Graham and De Clerk. His mission was to turn the company around after several years of declining profits.

"It's not very good, is it?" said Fergus.

"Neither side is really on form," said Scott. "Injuries, a string of bad results and falling confidence. Both sides are trying not to lose instead of trying to win." Scott hoped his clichéd analysis would pass muster with the new boss.

Fergus looked him in the eye and spoke slowly. "Scottish football is crap."

"Well, I can see how you might think that watching today's game."

"I've spent most of my life on the move. Living out of hotels and short-term lets. The opportunity to come back to Scotland was too good to pass up, but I'm not some misty-eyed ex-pat. This is crap. Look around the ground and tell me how many fans you think are here?"

"Two thousand."

"And how many do you think would buy it on pay-per-view TV?"

"Maybe another two thousand."

"If you're lucky. Probably a couple of hundred maximum."

Leave me alone, thought Scott. I need to think. I need to think about Lisa and Rob and how I'm going to stop from getting found out.

"Do you know when people are interested in Scottish football? When Rangers play Celtic, when the national side plays, and the occasional Champions League match."

"It's not as big as it was."

"Do you know what terrestrial TV is? It's mass market. It's nothing if it isn't mass market. The costs are too high for it to be anything else. We need a big audience day in, day out. Without that we can't sell advertising. Without advertising, we're finished. What's more, the people who really want to watch football have already seen the games on subscription channels."

"Why don't you just drop football?" snapped Scott.

"That would put you out of a job."

"So."

Now lying in bed on Sunday morning, Scott shook his head at the memory of it. He had practically talked himself out of job just to get Fergus to shut up and let him think. It had worked, Fergus stop talking for the rest of the match, but Scott still hadn't worked out what to do. His mind just kept circling round and round. Excuses being prepared. He couldn't stand it any longer. He had to speak to Lisa today and make sure she had no intention of confronting Rob.

***

"Yesterday was okay," said Lisa. "I mean, we were nice to each other, weren't we?"

"I know. We are too sarcastic with each other at times. Yesterday we weren't because we were at a funeral."

"Right, well let's try and have a good day without being at a funeral."

"Do you want to go to the art gallery?"

"No, not really. There's only so many times you can look at a stuffed elephant and find it interesting."

"Come on. We've not been there for ages. We could walk, have a quick look round and then go for lunch."

"Okay," said Lisa.

"I'm trying to do a bit of walking every day. Trying to get rid of some of this," he clutched a handful of stomach.

"Walking to the Kelvingrove will only burn a maximum of, say, 200 calories," said Lisa. "That's only slightly more than you get in a packet of crisps. You need to start running or going to the gym if you're serious. What do you think of Scott?" asked Lisa changing the subject as they left the house.

"In what way?"

"Well, is there an edge to your relationship?"

"We were in a band together, so yeah, I guess. There is always is. I wasn't as close to him as I was to the others, but Keith and I used to have huge fights, and we were very close, so it doesn't really mean anything."

"I've always found it strange that people can write songs together like you and Keith did. How can you split a song up?"

"I guess people do it in different ways, but sometimes one of us would come up with a melody that we couldn't do anything with, and the other person would take it over. Other times it was just a case of making minor changes. To be honest though, Keith and I didn't write together on the last album."

"So, who wrote the songs?"

"Both of us, but separately. Once you've matured as a musician and songwriter it's harder to share. You've got your own ideas."

"But you kept joint credits the same anyway?"

"We had a publishing deal and it just seemed easier."

"Wouldn't you feel guilty though if, say, Keith's songs were more successful than yours and you were taking half the money and half the credit? That doesn't seem right?"

Rob thought about it for a second. "Maybe, but I doubt it. We were a team and the arrangements were always a joint effort anyway."

"But if Keith had written all the songs you would have felt guilty?"

"That's a kind of bizarre question. Fancy grabbing a coffee for the way?"

"There goes that 200 calories in one latte."

"How would anyone know if only one of you had written all of the songs?" asked Lisa as they stood at the end of the bar waiting for their coffees.

Rob wasn't sure where this was going but was now getting irritated with it and had tried, unsuccessfully, to change the subject.

"Excuse me," said a man waiting next to them. "Sorry for eavesdropping, but it's kind of obvious."

"Sorry?" said Lisa.

"As they started writing separately, their songs had very distinct sounds, which wasn't the case in the earlier albums."

"Who are you?"

"Just a fan. Loved the last album. The name's Jim."

"Cheers," said Rob.

"No plans to do a solo tour?" he asked.

"Not at the moment, but maybe someday."

"I was at the last show. I remember you finishing up with 'Drunken Love'. That still gives me goose bumps when I hear it."

"It was a hard night."

"So, are you saying you can tell which songs Rob wrote and which ones Keith wrote?" Lisa asked.

"I couldn't get every one, but I reckon I would get most of them right."

"Do it then," she said.

"Okay. Right, do you want me to go through the album track by track or go through Rob's songs, then Keith's?"

"Does it matter?"

"Okay, I'll do it track by track. That way I'm less likely to miss any. Track number one, 'It's Got to Come Out', that is quite clearly Keith. Couple of little riffs that are a tribute to John Lee Hooker, classic Keith and integral to the song, so it has to be him."

"Just the songs and composer, or we'll be here all day," said Lisa.

"Right, sorry. Track two …"

\*\*\*

Scott paused for a few seconds before sending the text message. He stared at the screen of his mobile phone.

*Where are you?*

What if she was with Rob? They were colleagues and friends. Why shouldn't he be checking what they were doing? Maybe he was just checking to see if they wanted to go out for a drink.

He pressed the send button and it was gone.

Shouldn't have done it, he thought immediately. He put the phone down and stared out of the window.

You're a fool, he thought. You've got a life most people would envy and you're acting like a schoolboy with a crush.

The phone buzzed on the table. Scott grabbed it and read the reply.

*on way to kelvingrove art gallery with rob*

What did that mean? Did it mean Rob knew he'd texted? I need to just get this out of my system once and for all, he thought.

Scott pulled on a jacket and headed out of his flat. There was an entrance to Kelvingrove Park opposite. Rob and Lisa would be approaching from the other direction, so he was okay. No chance of bumping into them on the way. He headed down the hill and made his way towards the gallery.

Get this sorted and then see Fergus Veitch tomorrow, he thought. Veitch had been very quiet for the rest of the day after Scott had snapped at him. That was not a good position to be in. He brought a reputation with him as an axe man. The invite to the football match was a great opportunity. They had even shared a lift there and back. Scott had blown it. As the car dropped him off, Veitch's parting words to Scott were something along the lines of, "You've given me a lot to think about."

Scott reached the edge of the Park and stopped to look around, scanning the horizon for Rob and Lisa. Nothing.

Scott put his head down and walked quickly towards the art gallery. As he entered, he looked around. He couldn't see them, but it was busy. Lots of families milling around with parents chasing after their out of control children. Scott headed to the café in the central hall. He bought a coffee and sat down at one of the tables facing the entrance and tried to look as relaxed as possible. His eyes darted from face to face as a constant stream of people came through the doors. The sound of the concert organ started to echo round the building as the Sunday recital started. Scott recognised the tune. It was the one that the mad genius always played in old black and white horror movies.

Scott picked up a sheet of paper lying on the table detailing the recital. 'Organs at the Movies' was the title. It started with Bach's Toccata and Fugue in D Minor, from Phantom of the Opera.

Christ, he thought. Did they know I was coming? The tune played by the phantom after a hard day in the theatre, stalking the object of his desire. As if on cue, Rob and Lisa came through the entrance behind a family of four. Scott turned away while taking a sideways glance in their direction.

The phantom gets ready to pounce, he thought. If Rob knows I've texted, I should just breeze up and tell them I was bored and thought I'd join them. If he doesn't, I could try and see her alone. Scott looked round again, but they were gone. He stood up and headed towards the side gallery opposite, scanning as he went. The phantom on the prowl.

\*\*\*

Hugh took a bite of the roll. It tasted good, the perfect antidote for a hangover. He called it blood and guts. Square sausage, fried egg and a slice of black pudding. He had strolled down to the shop, bought a breakfast selection from the chill cabinet, a paper and a can of Coke. He then drank the Coke on the way back up the road to quench his hangover thirst. When he got home, he cooked breakfast, made a cup of tea and sat down in the living room to read the paper and watch TV.

A perfect Sunday morning. He was reading a story about a woman who had slept with a soap star only to find that he had filmed the whole thing. She had been so shocked when she found the tape that she had broken up with him and stolen all his videos. After checking the others to make sure she wasn't in any them, she discovered one in which his co-star in the soap appeared. It was then that she realised the world had to know what kind of man he was and that it was her duty to sell the story along with still photographs to the newspaper. Further pictures and an edited version of the video footage were available online. The story ended by explaining that she had donated half her fee to a charity of her choice. It didn't say which charity, just a charity of her choice. Hugh wondered how much she'd been paid for the story. More than a thousand pounds, he thought.

He took a drink of his tea and sat back. The TV program was some religious magazine. They were interviewing an Anglican priest who worked in Brazil. He was talking about his wife's kidnapping, or fake kidnapping to be more precise. He had received a phone call in which he could hear a woman crying in the background. The voice then told him his wife had been kidnapped and that he had to pay the equivalent of £2000 within the next hour to have her released. The priest knew it was fake because his wife was on holiday in England and was just off the phone to him before he received the kidnap call. These fake kidnappings were apparently very common in Brazil, practically an epidemic in the big cities. The priest then spoke about his faith and how it got him through the ordeal.

Hugh struggled to understand why it was an ordeal if the man knew his wife was back home in Seven Oaks. Two thousand pounds though, that was interesting. A ransom for as little as two thousand pounds. He supposed it must be a lot of money in Brazil, but still, it couldn't be life changing. If it's a fake kidnap though, that means you need to finish the whole thing off before the person realises it's fake. It needs to be small enough that they can just go to the bank straight away and take the money out, no questions asked.

Two thousand pounds would solve my problems, thought Hugh. It would solve my problems and leave enough left over for a holiday.

Hugh took another bite of his blood and guts roll and looked at the paper again and the story of the cheating soap star.

*Although what he did was wrong, I still miss the sex. He had stamina like no man I've ever known. I will never experience passion like that again, but I've still got the memories.*

Everywhere I look, he thought. She's making money, the Brazilian fake kidnappers are making money. Everyone apart from me is making money. He turned the page and read the next story.

My Wife Charged Me for Sex

Amazing Claim by Jilted Husband of Parish Councillor Escort.

\*\*\*

Lisa got the text from Scott as Rob was signing an autograph in the café. Rob did not notice her replying and she decided not to tell him. There was nothing to hide, but she couldn't see the point in mentioning it.

"So, did he get them all right?"

"No, but mostly. What sparked the interest in all this anyway?"

"I don't know. I was just thinking about how you never write anymore, and I suppose it just made me wonder how much of the band's material you wrote."

"I do still write. I have written a soundtrack."

"Yes, apart from that."

"And I think I'm going to do something with Orpheus Jones."

"This is the comic you are talking about?"

"Yes, the comic."

Lisa sighed. After all her efforts to try and get him to write, it would be ironic if he ended up producing some humiliating concept album based on a comic strip.

They walked in silence until they reached the art gallery. As they approached the entrance, they could hear the haunting sound of an organ. They entered the gallery and looked across the large hall to the far side, where the organ pipes dominated the space above the north entrance. Two children who had entered the building in front of them lifted both arms into a zombie position and began to walk in circles, legs straight, chasing each other.

"Anywhere you want to go first?" asked Rob.

"No, lead on." Lisa looked around the central hall, half expecting to see Scott. It was too busy to spot anyone, even if he was there.

They left the main hall and entered one of the side galleries. A bust of a Harpy greeted them, one talon-like hand clutching her breast, the other poised to strike anything that came within touching distance. Hanging from the ceiling were what looked like a hundred disembodied faces, each showing a different expression. Happiness, sadness, confusion, irritation.

Lisa looked down from the faces and rubbed the back of her neck. Off in the distance she saw Scott leaning out from behind a statue, spying on them. She looked round to see if Rob had noticed.

"Amazing, isn't it?" he said.

"Yes."

"Do you think every single one is different?"

"I think so yes. But there's so many of them."

"I know." He continued to look up.

Lisa glanced back to where Scott had been. She couldn't see him. She looked around the gallery. He was now behind a bust of William Wallace. He gave her a thumbs-up with raised eyebrows. Lisa had no idea what this meant but was certain he didn't want Rob to see him.

The music stopped and Rob turned to Lisa. "Do you want to go upstairs to the picture galleries?"

Lisa looked around. Scott had disappeared again. "Yes, why not."

As the organist started the next tune, the music began to echo through the gallery again.

"Listen to that?" said Rob. "Do you recognize it?"

"*Apocalypse Now*," she said. "'Flight of the Valkyrie'."

"Have you ever heard that played on a church organ before?"

"It is a good film, Rob, but the number of times I've watched it with you, I could never hear that tune again and it would be too soon."

Rob smiled. "I know, but a church organ. Let's go and have a listen."

"I need to go to the toilet. You go and listen, and I'll find you after."

They made their way back into the central hall, Lisa looking around the whole time. Rob sat at one the tables and picked up the recital sheet. Lisa carried on through the hall into the other wing. As she passed the stuffed Elephant, Scott appeared at her side.

"I'll meet you next to the dinosaur. Straight through here to the next gallery," he said. He then increased his pace turning left into a side gallery.

\*\*\*

"You can't be serious," said Kenny.

Hugh took a shot on the snooker table, hitting a red which then careered around the table before disturbing the pink. "These tables are too big. We should get pool tables in. At least you can finish a game on a pool table."

"Kidnapping?"

"Not a real kidnap. A fake kidnap. Two thousand quid. I pay off Jaffa and we head off to Magaluf for a week." Hugh took a drink of his lager.

"Shona would never let me go to Magaluf for a week with you."

"Don't tell her."

"We could do a weekend, but not a week. You can get cheap flights to Palma, out on Friday, back on Monday. I could tell her we were going to Blackpool."

"What about a weekend in Blackpool? We had a great time there last year."

"We did."

"So, it's Blackpool then?"

"Do you know how long you would get put away for if you kidnapped someone?"

"But that's the point, it wouldn't be a kidnapping, would it? What would you be charged with if you were caught? Kidding on?"

"Well, I suppose," said Kenny.

"That's the beauty of it. You haven't broken the law if you are caught. There's no risk."

"It must be against some kind of law."

"But it's just kidding on."

"Supposing we did it, is it Rob or his girlfriend we kidnap?"

"Pretend to kidnap," Hugh corrected.

"But which one?"

"Well, I've been thinking about that. I reckon you're more likely to get the money out of a woman than a man. In Brazil, it's nearly always mothers and wives that pay out. If that's what works, we should stick to that."

"So how do we go about it?"

"I've not worked out all the details, but what we need to do is get a recording of someone sounding like Rob to play in the background when we phone his girlfriend. I can do that. It doesn't need to be perfect, because she'll just hear it as a background noise."

"We could use Colin's mobile phone."

"I'm telling you, Kenny, this will work."

"When do we do it?"

"It needs to be this week. Jaffa wants his money on Friday. I reckon the quicker we do it the better. Before we lose our nerve."

"What times are the buses into Glasgow?" asked Kenny.

"We are not getting the bus to a kidnapping. We need to borrow some wheels."

"A fake kidnapping," said Kenny.

"Yeah, a fake kidnapping."

***

Lisa stopped in front of the dinosaur and looked around. Scott was nowhere to be seen.

He must be losing his mind, she thought. She looked over towards the skeleton of a deer or some other animal.

"Does he know I'm here?"

Lisa jumped and turned to find Scott standing next to her. "God, what are you doing?"

"Does he?"

"No, unless he's seen you. Why all the cloak and dagger?"

"I didn't want a confrontation."

"What are you talking about?"

"Where's Rob?" Scott looked around.

"Relax, he's listening to the organ music."

"How long have we got?"

"For God's sake," said Lisa. "Come on. We'll go to the Halycon for lunch. I can't stand this place anyway."

"What about Rob, you can't just leave him here."

"We were going there anyway. He can catch up."

"Wait here. I'll go first. I'll meet you at the bus stop outside."

"No," said Lisa. "If we're going, we're going. Come on."

Lisa turned and headed back through the gallery containing stuffed animals and out into the central hall again. Scott followed on behind. Lisa saw Rob sitting facing the other way, looking up towards the organ.

Probably got his eyes closed, she thought. A dreamer and a layabout, ever since she'd known him. Walking towards the entrance, Lisa knew she was making a decision. It was time to leave him. Not today perhaps, but soon. The whole thing had run its course.

"I wanted to make sure that you hadn't said anything to Rob," said Scott after they were clear of the building and making their way towards the Halycon.

"Is that it Is that the important thing you wanted to say?"

"It's important, Lisa. There's no proof, you know. It would just be my word against his. What would it gain?"

"Well no, I haven't said anything to him. We did have a conversation about song-writing today though, and I was assured that it was obvious there were two separate writers on the last album."

"He said that. Why did you ask him about that? What did he say?"

"Not him, it was a stranger."

"Who?"

Lisa explained the encounter in the café. Scott was nervous, which made Lisa certain he had been lying to her.

"You see. No one would believe it. Keith was a fantastic mimic. Do you know what he used to do? We would name a band, and he would write a song in their style within half an hour. He used to joke that the only band he couldn't do was Oasis, because it always ended up sounding like the Beatles."

"So, you're saying that Keith sometimes copied Rob's style? The later stuff that sounded like Rob was actually Keith?"

"Yeah, basically."

"Well, that's quite a story, Scott, but you didn't need to stalk me to stop me from confronting Rob about it."

"That wasn't the only reason. I wanted to see you, wanted to spend some time alone with you."

Lisa regretting asking but felt compelled to do so. "Why?" she asked.

***

Hugh's mother had invited him over for Sunday lunch when they had been at the funeral the day before. She was off on a bus tour of the Highlands on Monday. Hugh assumed that he was getting the keys to the house handed over and a list of tasks to do while she was away.

As he approached the house, he spotted Steve's car parked outside the house. Steve was his mother's latest friend.

"Hi Mum."

"Have a seat, Hugh, lunch won't be ready for a while yet."

Hugh heard the toilet flushing. "Steve?"

"Yes, he's staying for lunch."

"Is he?"

Hugh's mother went through to the kitchen to continue making the lunch. Hugh sat down and picked up the paper.

"Alright, young man?" said Steve as he entered the living room.

"Yeah," Hugh looked up at him. He was in his mid-seventies but still had jet-black hair, slicked back. Worse than that, he wore a V-necked jumper with nothing on underneath it. His bare chest covered in grey hairs proclaimed to the world that he was still a player. A gold rope chain round his neck and a signet ring on his finger with the intertwined letters of Rangers Football Club, R.F.C. He made Hugh's skin crawl.

"Want a beer, Shagger?"

"Yeah," said Hugh, trying not to get drawn into conversation with him.

Steve went through to the kitchen.

"Hey, hands off, Mr Skelton," said Hugh's mother.

Hugh's mood blackened further. He imagined Steve Scumbag fondling his mother behind the kitchen door.

"Looking good," said Steve as he returned with two beers. "Your mother can cook. I'll say that for her."

Hugh opened the beer and took a drink. He had to stop imagining Steve with his mother. It was crazy. Even if they did end up together, so what? That was his mother's business, not Hugh's. She was entitled to a little happiness and fun. But the thought of Steve and his mother kissing, it was just wrong. Why couldn't they lay off the whole sex thing? Hugh remembered his grandparents having single beds, and that was before they were even retired. They were younger than his mother and Steve.

"So, Mum's off on one of her trips tomorrow," said Hugh.

"I'm going with her, Shagger. Did your mother not tell you?"

"No, she didn't, Steve."

"First time she's invited me along. I guess she's just a bit embarrassed about saying. You don't have a problem about that, do you?"

Hugh paused before answering. "No, I suppose not. Wouldn't have thought it was your cup of tea though. Bus trips to Lochs and Castles."

"It's not really, but we'll have a good time at night."

Hugh couldn't help himself. He had a vision of his mother and Steve making love, loose skin sliding everywhere as they tried to get a grip on each other. He grimaced and shook his head.

"No, son. I didn't mean like that," said Steve, noticing the look of disgust on Hugh's face. "I meant we'll have dinner, have a few drinks with friends, and they lay on a dance on every night. Listen, I was wondering if you could come with us down to Hamilton tomorrow, then bring the car back up the road for me?"

"I suppose," said Hugh.

"You've got a license, haven't you? The tour leaves from Hamilton Bus Station."

"Yeah, okay, but I was going to go into Glasgow tomorrow. Would you mind if I use the car afterwards?"

"Feel free, son. Treat it as your own while I'm away."

"Okay."

The image of his mother making love to Steve, now replaced by one of Hugh driving into town with Kenny at his side. Six degrees of separation, he thought. It's not just about who you want to be connected to. It's who you are actually connected to. Hugh smiled as he imagined writing up his Back to Work homework as a list of people who could help him with the kidnapping. Not what the course tutor had in mind, but Hugh was finding the skills he'd learnt very useful.

"Do you want another beer, Steve?"

\*\*\*

Rob had circled round the art gallery a couple of times but couldn't see Lisa anywhere. He then went back to the central hall and sat there for a while, thinking that she might be looking for him. Best thing to do was to stay in the same place and hopefully she would find him. Eventually he concluded that she had left without trying to find him. He reckoned she would have just headed straight for the Halycon, so he left to make his way there.

Rob thought about the Orpheus Jones story. He could understand why Lisa didn't get it, lots of people couldn't see comics as anything other than childish, but all the same it annoyed him. When he had done the soundtrack, she was the same. She saw it as tinkering rather than work. Rob had met Lisa after the band had split up, so she probably had some vision of a wildly energetic creative period, but it had never been like that for Rob. Creativity for him had always been slow and drifting. Ideas came out of periods of torpor. They had never been forged in the white heat of activity. One of Rob's favourite sayings was a Spanish saying he'd come across, *'Que bonito es no hacer nada, y luego descansar'*. 'How beautiful it is to do nothing, and then to rest.' That described exactly how Rob was at his most creative.

When they had first started seeing each other, one of the things he had liked about her was the way that she was so unimpressed by him. She was not a fan of the band, had never seen them, she didn't even know many of the songs. If he was honest, Rob didn't show much interest in Lisa's career either. He found the whole notion of being a television presenter without any kind of specialist knowledge ridiculous. What we need is more eccentric experts presenting in their area of interest, that's entertaining, he thought. Rob tried to remember the name of the old lady in tweed skirts who used to present a dog training program. Barbara something. Mad as a hatter, but she knew her stuff, and her behaviour and mannerisms were so out of the ordinary that she ended up having a cult following. That scientist, he was the same, what was his name? Magnus Pike, arms waving around, as his face contorted with the effort of explaining the importance of what he was talking about. They were real presenters. That was before presenters became customer sales reps. They sound good, but they're just following a script, and where is the authenticity in that? People like authenticity, they recognize it, even now in an age of image. Take away the script and what's left?

"Do you know if Lisa Ward is in?" Rob asked the receptionist at the Halycon.

"Yes sir, she's in the restaurant."

Rob made his way through the club and found Lisa sharing a drink and meal with Scott.

"Rob, there you are. I couldn't find you, so I thought I'd just meet you here. It's about time you joined the modern world and got yourself a mobile phone."

"You can get me one for Christmas".

"Hi Rob," said Scott nervously. "I just met Lisa here."

"Where else would you have met her?" said Rob. "Listen, do you remember Magnus Pike, the TV scientist?"

"Used to wave his arms around," said Scott.

"That's him. And what was that woman who trained the dogs called? Old woman wore tweed skirts and used to shout 'walkies!' all the time. Barbara something?"

"Barbara Woodhouse," said Lisa.

"That's it, Barbara Woodhouse. I was just thinking about the two of them. You don't get people like that on TV these days."

Lisa smiled. "I know. TV is a lot more professional these days. It used to be so amateurish."

***

Scott had tried to stay cool with Lisa, but he had failed miserably. He told her how he felt about her and how he wanted to be with her. Everything came spilling out before Rob arrived. Lisa had sat there not saying much and somehow Scott felt obliged to fill the gap. Before he knew it, he had told her he loved her. The thought of her leaving him behind in Glasgow was breaking his heart. Lisa listened without replying and Scott ended up filling in the gaps again and again.

"What is it you want from me?" she finally asked.

"I've told you. What else is there to say?" he replied. Lisa appeared completely composed and unaffected by everything he had told her. "What about you Lisa? How do you feel about me?"

"To be honest, I've never given it much thought." Lisa paused for a moment as if rolling the idea around a little. "We would be good together in a lot of ways. We understand each other's work. Rob doesn't really value what I do. He's never said that, but it's obvious really."

"You two shouldn't be together."

"But I'm just not sure it would be a step forward if I got together with you. It's kind of like the girl who can't see beyond the end of her street. Do you know what I mean?"

"Not really," said Scott. Lisa seemed to be judging his declaration of love like a business proposal. He had worried about making a fool of himself, about being rejected, even that she might laugh at him, but this? This was something he hadn't expected. He felt as though he was in a negotiation.

"Well, you know. Lisa Ward and the guy from that band, Lisa Ward and the other guy from that band. That kind of thing."

"I'll be there for you in a way that Rob never would," said Scott, embarrassed with himself for joining in the negotiation, but unable to help himself.

"It could also be seen as a little seedy."

"I don't see why."

"Here comes Rob."

"I'll bet you any money," said Rob, "that Barbara Woodhouse got better viewing figures than most of today's so-called celebrities."

"Like who? Who are you talking about exactly?" said Lisa.

"Everyone got better viewing figures then," said Scott.

"We're all experts, aren't we?"

"No," said Scott. "I just meant that there were less channels, less choice. That's the problem today. The audience is split too many ways. TV is segmenting itself out of profitability," he said, repeating something that Fergus Veitch had told him the previous day.

"I suppose that's true," said Rob.

"Add the internet into the mix and TV has got real problems. The cost of putting out content hasn't gone down, but advertising revenue has."

"So, what's the answer?"

"Consolidation of ownership. Re-use of material on digital channels, web delivery of content. Roll all the advertising across the different channels and sell it as a package."

Rob nodded. "Makes sense. You could get all those old programs available online. Barbara Woodhouse, Magnus Pike. People could watch them whenever they like. Look at all those nostalgia shows. There must still be a market for it."

Scott was relieved to be discussing the problems of the TV industry in the internet age. He was back on solid ground.

Lisa sat back and fumed. Rob was getting at her again. Why had he gone on about Barbara Woodhouse, a pet presenter, and what the hell was Scott on about? Since when had he been interested in advertising revenue?

"Listen to you," said Lisa. "The TV expert. Bring back Barbara Woodhouse, she wouldn't last a minute. We make it look easy but believe me it's not. You should know that, Scott. The very first program you presented, you made one mistake and people still joke about it two years later."

Scott face reddened at the memory of it. Dundee had been playing Dundee United in the cup. He got the result the wrong way around and then stumbled over the correction misnaming Dundee as Dundee City. It was the one mistake he'd ever made, but Lisa was right, people still mentioned it with relish. It had even made it on to a sketch show with an impressionist playing Scott saying 'Dundee Academical versus Dundee Rovers'.

"It's ridiculous a city the size of Dundee having two football clubs anyway," said Scott. "Two grounds within sight of each other."

"There's always going to be room for authenticity," said Rob. "Not everything has to be slick."

"Who are you talking about, Rob? Give us an example."

"I'm not making a point about any individual. I'm talking about the trend towards superficiality."

Lisa leaned forward and spoke in a quiet but firm voice. "The fuck you are."

"Where did that come from?"

"You come in here talking about Barbara fucking Woodlouse, dog trainer. Dog trainer! What am I waiting to hear about? A program based on pets. She was this, she was that, she was authentic. You might as well come right out and say it."

"What are you talking about?"

"You know exactly what I mean," Lisa hissed. "I'll tell you something she wasn't. She probably wasn't a fan of comic books. She was an adult. Not a child."

"You know what, Lisa? You're right. It sounds as if I'm getting at you. I didn't think about it. But maybe you're right. I don't think that pet cemetery or whatever it is, sounds that great. I don't think it's something you have any real interest or knowledge in and the idea of you getting your face on dog food? Why would you even want it? Why?"

"Fuck face," said Lisa. "Total fuck face."

"Does anyone want another drink?" asked Scott. He had no idea how things had escalated out of control so quickly, and it was the only thing he could think of to say.

"Yes, Scott, I'll have a whisky, Highland Park."

"To drown out the fact that you are a talentless shit," said Lisa.

"And you, Lisa? What do you want?"

"Who hasn't written a thing in four years, assuming that he wrote anything before then?"

"Right. I get it. That's what all the questions were about. So, I didn't write any of the Delta's songs. Is that it?"

"That's it, Lanarkshire man! Mr Authenticity. Willing to sit in the West End of Glasgow being a big fish in a small pond. Criticises anyone who steps out and measures themselves against the wider world."

"Maybe I should leave you two alone," said Scott.

"Sure, Scott. We shouldn't be having this conversation in front of you."

"Stay where you are," said Lisa. "See this guy here?" she pointed at Scott. "He's picked himself up, dusted himself down and got on with the rest of his life after the band broke up. He's made a career for himself. You weren't just getting at me. You were getting at him too."

"Wait a minute. Don't bring other people into it."

"Jack, he's gone and worked in other people's restaurants to build up his experience and now he's opening his own. He's got on with his life. What do you do? You drink beer, eat nuts and watch movies in a room surrounded by gold and platinum discs from your past. It's pathetic."

"Discs that you put up," said Rob. "Not me."

"I'll just go and order the drinks."

## Chapter 5

Scott woke up early. He stretched and moved his neck left and right loosening it off. He sat up and leaned his head back then forward. The couch was not designed for sleeping on. He looked over towards his bedroom.

After leaving the Halcyon, Scott invited Lisa back to his place. She agreed. Unfortunately, she then spent the rest of the night talking about Rob and recounting in great detail every occasion that he had ever talked her and her career down. She then, quite suddenly, said she needed to go to bed and asked where she was sleeping. Although Scott's flat was spacious, it only had one bedroom, so he did the decent thing and offered her his bed.

"I'll sleep on the couch," he said.

"Well obviously. Have you got a change of sheets?"

It wasn't exactly how he'd imagined his first night with Lisa, but she was here in his flat. She was not going back to Rob, so he went to sleep happy. Things were moving in his direction.

Scott got up and made some breakfast for Lisa. Putting it on a tray he took it through to the bedroom, where he was confronted by an empty bed. The sheets and pillowcases she had used had been stripped from the bed and folded up. Scott sat down and read the note thanking him for his support. It also asked him not to mention to anyone that she had stayed the night with him.

After arriving at work he tracked down her in the canteen. "Why did you leave so early?" he asked sitting down.

"I didn't want to disturb you."

"It's no problem. You're welcome. You can stay as long as you want."

"Thanks for the offer, but I don't think it would be appropriate."

"What are you going to do?"

"I've not decided."

"Are you going back to him?" he asked, amazed that she would consider it after the row that he'd witnessed.

"No, but I do have options, Scott. My world does not revolve around having a man to stay with or having this job here for that matter."

"I didn't mean …"

"I have my own place. I just didn't have the keys with me. I won't be phoning the women's refuge just yet."

Scott was confused. Lisa's anger towards Rob seemed to be heading in his direction. He decided it was time to make a tactical retreat.

"I just wanted you to know that there was help for you if you need it. That's all."

"Have you checked your email yet?"

"No, I've just arrived. Why?"

"Well I suggest you do. I've never seen anything like it. I don't know how he thinks he can get away with something like that. I certainly won't be begging to stay."

Scott made his way towards his office, wondering why Rob would send them an email. She had not mentioned Rob, but he assumed the email was from him.

"Have you read your email yet?" asked another fellow presenter as he passed in the corridor.

"Not yet," said Scott. "Did you get one from him?"

"Everyone did. Everyone. Can you believe it?"

***

Rob woke up to the sound of silence. He looked at the clock on the bedside unit. 8:30 a.m. It was earlier than he'd woken for weeks. He headed downstairs for breakfast, listening to the silence all the way. It was stupid really. The house was always silent when he woke up. Lisa left for work long before he got up. But today was different. Today it was really silent. There were no memories of night-time arguments. No lingering mood of conflict. It felt good.

Rob wondered where Lisa had spent the night. She had gone off with Scott after they left the Halcyon with the parting shot of 'Fuck you, comic boy'. Rob laughed at the memory of it. Lisa would never get the point of graphic novels, but then he would never get the point of daytime TV. He was sure that he would feel sad at the demise of their relationship at some point, but right now all he felt was relief.

Rob poured himself a coffee and sorted through some more of the pictures from Orpheus Jones. He singled out a scene showing Orpheus sitting in an armchair watching TV in the dark. The room in the scene vibrated slightly, and the next picture showed the building Orpheus was sitting in. It was a cross section view of the building and the ground below. A tube train passed underneath. After the train had gone Orpheus continued to shake even though the room was now still. His shaking became more violent until he snapped, stood up and threw a lamp at the TV, smashing the screen. Another song, another stage in the story for Rob to work on. This, he decided, was what he would be putting his time and energy into for the foreseeable future.

Rob rifled through a couple of kitchen drawers and eventually found what he was looking for. Flicking through the address book he found Frank McCusker's number and punched the numbers into the phone.

"Mmh," said the voice on the other end.

"Frank?"

"Mmh, what? Who is this?"

"It's Rob Young here."

"Who? Oh Rob, what time is it?"

"Did I wake you up?"

"If it's before ten, yes. What is it?"

"I wanted to chat about Orpheus Jones."

"Christ, you are joking, aren't you?"

"Not right now. I mean I want to meet up and talk about it."

"I'm not into book groups, Rob, but thanks for the invite."

"I want to do something with it."

"What did you have in mind?" asked Frank, beginning to sound more awake and interested.

"I don't know. That's what I wanted to talk to you about. Maybe an album, maybe a show, but I don't want to take it any further without talking to you about it first. There's no point me spending time on it if you're not going to give your permission."

"Sounds like you've already done some work on it."

"Not much," Rob looked down at the two small piles of pictures on the kitchen table. "I've been dividing the story into themes, denial, rage, that kind of thing."

"Cool. The five stages of grief. Not everyone gets that, you know. I thought it was too obvious when I wrote it. You're one of the few people to ever mention it to me. Christ, that's what the Orpheus myth was about. It even had bargaining at the heart of the story. How much more obvious could it get?"

"Exactly," said Rob, writing a note across the phone book page as he spoke.

"Okay, let's meet up."

"What about tomorrow night?" My friend is opening a restaurant. Why not come along?"

When Rob put the phone down he read the scribbled note. After pouring another coffee he headed through to the study to Google 'five stages of grief'.

***

"There you go," said Rab as he handed Scott a sheet of paper and sat down next to him in the canteen.

*Dear Fergus,*

*You should keep me at the station because 'Show Us Your Balls' has the best ratings of any of our own productions. I devised the show, I write the script, I present it. Without me there is no show.*

*Regards,*

*Rab*

"Is that it?" asked Scott.

"What else is there to say? I've got good ratings, end of story."

"I'm not sure what to say in mine."

"Relax, he can't get rid of football. It's Scotland."

"I'm not so sure, and besides, it's not the show we have to justify it's our own position."

Two hours earlier Fergus Veitch had sent out an email to every presenter at the station asking them to reply by the end of the day, explaining in no more than two hundred words why they should be kept on. He had explained in considerably more than two hundred words what a difficult position the company was in, and that it was now time to cut adrift anyone not paying their way. Since the email had gone out, Scott had tried without much success to find out what people were saying in reply. Only Rab had been willing to openly discuss it. The printed reply he showed Scott had been written within ten minutes of Veitch sending his email out.

"He can get rid of me if he wants," said Rab. "But I am the best-rated show. I checked it out. Not even 'Murder Polis' beats me. This is a footballing nation, Scott."

"I went to the Motherwell match at the weekend with him. He wasn't too impressed."

"Yeah well, the first mistake you made there was going to Motherwell."

"I'm telling you, Rab, he doesn't rate it."

"Who would? We are a footballing nation, but that doesn't mean we're any good at it. We still enjoy talking about it though, and that's where I come in."

"What will you do if he sacks you?"

"He won't. But if he did, I'd go over to the other side. I got an offer a couple of months ago. I reckon the it would still be open."

"I suppose you'd still have the newspaper column and radio slot as well."

Rab laughed. "It does help if you're not desperate, that's for sure."

"I'm not sure what to say to him."

"Tell him that no Dundee United versus Dundee Hotspur game would be the same without your incisive analysis." Rab laughed at his own joke.

"The ratings haven't been that great and I actually told him on Saturday that he should drop football from the schedule."

Rab roared with laughter. "Jesus Scott, we all feel like that when we watch Motherwell. The secret is not to say it out loud when you're with the boss."

"I don't think football is my thing if I'm honest."

"You think?" said Rab sarcastically. "Look, don't be so hard on yourself. Every football presenter I've known is rubbish. If they were any good, they'd be working in the game, not talking about it."

"Thanks, Rab," said Scott.

*Fergus,*

*I wish I could think of a reason that you should keep me on as a sports presenter, but if I'm honest, I can't. Football is Scotland's national sport, but you're right, there are only certain games that are of interest to a large audience. I've enjoyed my time at the station but if it's time to move on, so be it.*

*Yours,*

*Scott*

Scott's finger hovered over the mouse button as he read and re-read the email. Lisa was heading south and maybe it was time for him to move on too. He could get some TV work on one of the cable channels as last resort. What the hell. Scott hit the send button.

\*\*\*

Denial, anger, bargaining, depression and acceptance. The five stages of grief lay before Rob on the screen.

Orpheus Jones did indeed match the stages quite closely. After the denial and anger Orpheus inhabited the Tube searching for his love. One night he found a doorway that lead to service tunnels. In these he found the spirits of the dead, living in a half-world. In the world, but not part of it. This was how Orpheus felt without his partner and he enlisted the help of friendly spirits to roam the underground looking for her.

Rob thought about the death of both his mother and Keith. They came within a year of each other, his mother first then within months, Keith's accident. Jack's father had also died in the same period. The band had felt surrounded and immersed in grief. Rob wasn't sure whether he had experienced the five stages or not. One period of grief had been overtaken by another. After the band had split, he couldn't even bear to listen to their music anymore.

The farewell concert had not given what so-called experts referred to as closure. How could it when it took place within weeks of Keith's death? Closure, Rob thought, happens over a much longer period. Closure comes when you can think about and talk about the person you've lost without the pain of their loss crowding out all other memories. Rob hadn't been grieving for four years, but he hadn't exactly moved on either. He had done the movie soundtrack, but by his own standards he had been semi-retired. Now that time had come to an end and he was ready to be productive again.

Rob pulled a pile of blank sheets out of the printer and headed back through to the kitchen. He placed five sheets on the table and wrote one of the stages of grief on each. Rob was now ready to work. The thought of Lisa sitting on the edge of the bed on the morning of the funeral intruded into his thoughts. She looked beautiful that morning. Rob remembered the desire to pull her back into bed and make love to her. Perhaps they just needed some time apart, a trial separation. He shook his head and began sifting through the pictures placing them on the appropriate sheet. Who was he kidding? She had spurned every physical advance he'd made towards her for weeks. What about the way she just left him at the museum? And then there was the memory of her face, contorted by hate, practically spitting venom at him in the Halycon. There was no point in fooling himself, it was over. Rob sighed and shook his head again. He put some more coffee on to brew and stared out the window. How had it come to this? It doesn't matter how, he thought, carrying on the internal dialogue. This is the way it is, and I need to just move on, end of story. Catching sight of his reflection in the window he decided it was time to get that haircut finished.

***

Lisa flicked through the paper, searching for the story. She had hoped it would be on the front page, but unfortunately a story about a Polish women claiming British child benefit despite having moved back to Krakow was splashed across the front page. It shared space with an advert for a free CD of power ballads.

Lisa eventually found it on page seven.

Barton Plays Away with Lookalike Lover

*Premiership footballer Jason Barton may only be playing a bit part for his club this season, but he has shown he's more than capable of scoring away from home.*

Lisa looked at the picture of Zoe Barton, ex-Miss Great Britain and one of Lisa's rivals for the Doghouse Makeover slot. Zoe was shown pushing past photographers.

After receiving the email from Fergus Vietch, Lisa had picked up the phone and contacted her agent.

"I need to know what's happening with the job. Is there any news?" she had asked.

"I told you, it will be later in the week. However, there is some good news," he said. "Zoe Barton is in the paper and not in a good way. That narrows the field down to two."

Lisa had gone to the front desk at reception and picked up a copy of the paper. Now sitting in the office, she read the story.

*Barton has adopted a system of playing two up-front by taking his wife and girlfriend to the same restaurants and nightclubs. He has managed to get away it up till now because his girlfriend is a dead ringer for his wife, ex-Miss Great Britain, Zoe Barton.*

*Secret girlfriend, Rachel Sheppard was encouraged to dress up like Zoe in case anyone saw them. 'He even used to call me Zoe when we were out together,' said a tearful Rachel as she revealed the truth behind Barton's away game tactics.*

Lisa stared at the pictures of the two women. They looked like twins. Why would he have an affair with someone who looked just like his partner? Lisa phoned her agent back.

"I don't get it," said Lisa.

"In what way?"

"Why that rules her out of the job. If she was having an affair, then I could understand it. It's her husband that's been cheating on her."

"Two words, Lisa - daytime TV. It's a different world. God knows why, but it is. The slightest whiff of scandal and that's you. If she already had the job, she would have been fine, but when she's competing for a job, it's the kiss of death."

"So, you think she's out of the running then?"

"She's toast, Lisa. I've spoken to the producer this morning. His words were that she's done nothing wrong, but he doesn't want anything to distract from the show."

"God, that's terrible."

"Let's get the job and then feel sorry for her, Lisa."

"When?"

"Sometime this week. I can't tell you any more than that. I know it's frustrating."

Lisa explained about the email from Fergus and how she didn't want to grovel for her job if she already had another lined up. Her agent went quiet on the other end of the phone.

"Are you still there?"

"Just thinking, Lisa. We don't want you unemployed. Would you employ someone who's been sacked?"

"It depends on the circumstances."

"Wrong answer. Everyone will think, 'Well, if they didn't want her, why should I? What's wrong with her? What do they know?' You haven't replied to the email yet, have you?"

"No, not yet. That's why I phoned you."

"Good. Fight for your job. Lisa Ward, the one presenter they knew they had to keep. That's what I want to be telling producers. Understood?"

Lisa composed her email cutting and refining to get as much as she could into the two hundred words. She explained that not only did she love her current job, but that she loved the station and would be willing to work where required to help pull the station through the current difficulties. She acknowledged that she did have other possibilities, everyone knew she did, and it would appear odd not to mention them. If she was with the station, however, she would give one hundred and ten percent. Lisa toyed with making it two hundred percent, but on reflection felt that one hundred and ten was more believable.

***

The hair salon was in darkness as Rob approached. The opening hours were etched on the door. Closed Monday. Rob was about to head off back home when he spotted a light at the back of the shop. He pressed his face up against the tinted windows and peered in. A door was lying open into an office or kitchen. Rob took a chance and knocked the window. A face peered round the door. He couldn't quite make it out but waved. The person disappeared back behind the door before emerging, keys in hand. It was Kate. She smiled as she walked over to the door and unlocked it.

"Pitside," Rob said.

"Pitside?"

"That's where we met. Pitside. We danced to Japan and then the halfwit threw up over us."

Kate liked the fact that he hadn't mentioned Hugh by name. "I thought he only caught me when he threw up."

"So, any chance of a haircut?"

"We're closed today."

"What are you doing?"

"Bookkeeping. It's the only day I get a chance."

"Wouldn't take long."

Kate opened the door wide and motioned him in.

"Put this on and have a seat," said Kate handing him a gown.

"So, is this your place?"

"Yes."

"When did you leave Pitside?"

"As soon as I could, but not soon enough."

"I was out that way on Saturday. I was at a funeral in Rigburn. An uncle of mine."

"Was Hugh there?"

"Oh yeah. He asked me for a loan. That's why I remembered you."

"Oh thanks."

"No, I didn't mean it like that."

"What was the loan for?"

"Who knows? What's it ever for?"

"I stopped seeing him the day after that disco, you know."

"I'm not surprised. He can be good company at times, but it's just not worth it, is it?"

"Shagger. That's his nickname. Ever since that night."

"Why?"

Kate found herself recounting the night to Rob. He'd forgotten many of the details and did not remember Hugh's shouted boast as he was led from the hall. Kate found herself laughing as she described the events of that night long ago. The fact that Rob had not found them memorable enough to recall somehow meant she didn't feel defensive about them.

"I guess you don't see much of him nowadays?" asked Rob.

"More than I would like to. My sister is married to his friend. When I visit her, he's quite often around. Last time I saw him he borrowed a tenner from me, but it was worth it to get rid of him. So, what am I doing with this hair?"

"Anything you want. I feel like a change. A new start."

Kate looked at him in the mirror facing them. "Do you want the grey coloured?"

"God no."

"You should get it shorter then."

"Go for it."

"Much shorter."

"As long as you don't scalp me, you can do what you want."

"Well that makes it easy. Are you trying to disguise yourself or something?"

"No, I just feel like a change, that's all."

Rob found himself talking about the previous day's events including the argument in the Halycon.

"So, is she seeing Scott?"

"No, that was just a coincidence, bumping into him."

"Oh,"

"You don't think it was a coincidence?"

"I have absolutely no idea or opinion about it. I just thought that's what you meant."

"I don't think they are. Does it sound as if they are?"

"I don't know, I mean no."

"I suppose they could be," said Rob. "They see a lot of each other. Maybe they are."

"Look, I just probably picked you up wrong. Ignore me."

"How did I not see that?"

\*\*\*

"Can't it go any faster?" asked Kenny.

"My foot is flat on the floor," said Hugh.

"Fifty miles an hour, that can't be right. Are you in fifth gear?"

"Yeah, it's wrecked."

Hugh and Kenny were heading into Glasgow after dropping off Hugh's mother at the bus station in Hamilton. Steve had driven from Pitside to Hamilton with Hugh sitting alongside him getting notes on the peculiarities of the car as they went. Steve had explained how the accelerator had to be fully depressed before turning the ignition keys. The trick was to turn the key, holding it for a second or two before beginning to pump the accelerator. If you got it wrong and flooded the engine, it would usually fix itself if you left it for five minutes then did the same again. As they left the street, Steve explained how the second gear didn't work. The trick to jumping from first to third was to over-rev the engine just as you put your foot down on the clutch pedal.

"He's probably hoping you crash it, so that he can claim the insurance," said Kenny.

"I can't stand that guy."

"Is he and your mum, you know?"

"Kenny, some things are off limits, and that's one of them."

"Fair enough. It doesn't really bear thinking about, does it?"

"It doesn't," said Hugh.

"Did you see his trousers, all covered in Christ-knows what kind of stains."

"The driver's seat was still warm when I sat down."

"Imagine sleeping with him," said Kenny. "Imagine being the woman that goes …"

"Kenny?"

"What?"

"Shut up, will you?"

"Sorry Shagger. It was just when you described the seat being all hot and sweaty.

It kind of conjures up an image."

"I didn't say it was sweaty. Do you think I would be sitting here if it was sweaty?"

"I couldn't stand the thought of him with my mum."

"Kenny."

"I know, I know. I can't help it. The guy is sleazy. He looks like the kind of guy who doesn't clean his cock between shags."

"Kenny, I swear to God if you don't stop talking about him, I'm going to drive this car off the road."

After driving in silence for the rest of the journey they reached Glasgow and took the cut-off for the West End, Kenny giving directions as they went. Twenty minutes later they found themselves driving in first gear past Rob's house. They kept driving and parked a short distance along the street, just out of view.

"So, you take him out for a drink, and I call the house?" said Kenny.

"Yep. I think we passed a phone box about a hundred yards back. You play the recording and read the script."

Kenny pulled the mobile phone and a scrap of paper out of his pocket. He opened the paper and read it silently.

"You okay?"

"I don't know, Shagger. This doesn't feel right."

"It'll be okay. The recording sounds good."

"I know, but what if she calls the police?"

"Don't start panicking on me, Kenny. If we stay calm, it'll work. If we panic, it won't."

"Right, do it before I change my mind," Kenny shook his head.

"Okay." Hugh reached into his pocket and pulled out the beer mat with the address and telephone number. "I'll phone from the call box. That way there's no record linking your phone."

"Colin's phone. My son's phone." Kenny shook his head again.

"Kenny don't start. I'm nervous too."

"Is the tax disc up to date?"

"Why would that make any difference?" said Hugh, beginning to lose his temper.

"Look in the rear mirror."

A traffic warden was approaching the car.

"Shit." Hugh wound down his window. "Is there a problem?"

"Resident's permits only," said the warden. "You can't park here, unless you're just dropping something off."

"I'm visiting a friend."

"I'm afraid it doesn't matter. Your nearest parking is just off Byres Road."

"I'll just let my friend know we're here."

"And I'll just write you a ticket if you don't move on."

"You're joking?"

"I'm not, move on."

Hugh wound up his window, put his foot down on the accelerator and turned the ignition key.

"Remember to pump," said Kenny.

***

Rob knocked on a locked door for the second time that day.

"Are you sure he won't mind?" asked Kate.

They were standing outside Fratello Scozia, Jack's new restaurant.

"Here he comes."

"Christ, who scalped you?" said Jack as he opened the door.

"She did." Rob pointed at Kate.

"Only joking, it's about time he got a haircut," Jack backtracked.

"This is Kate. An old friend from way back. We were passing by and I thought I'd pop in for a preview. Is that okay?"

"Of course it is, come in." Jack ushered them through to the restaurant.

"You ready for tomorrow, Jack?"

"Yeah. What do you think then? We've taken some tables out to make space for the band, but this is it."

"It looks good."

"That's based on the old Tennent's lager cans," said Kate pointing to a picture on the wall above one of the booths.

The picture was of a lager can. There was T logo in the corner and the can had a photograph with a blue trim on it. The photograph was of an old woman walking across a pebble beach. She had a headscarf on and was carrying a handbag. In the lower left-hand corner of the photograph was the word 'Granny'.

"It is," said Jack. "Remember the 'lager lovelies'? Pictures of models on the back of Tennent's lager cans in the seventies? This is a play on that. The seven ages of lager lovelies."

"That's clever," said Kate. "Who did them?"

"I did all the artwork," said Jack. "Look, this one over here is based on a Tunnock's Tea cake wrapper."

The picture showed a large red circle on a silver background with red lettering surrounding the centre circle. The whole thing had rays of red lines emanating out towards the edges, like sunbeams.

Kate leaned in close and read the words out loud. "So queer the moonlight she felt the running of that beam along her back. And she straightened as the moonlight grew and looked at the rest of herself and thought herself sweet and cool."

"This is all from my Andy Warhol phase at Art School," said Jack. "Never went down well with the tutors. But there you go. I've found a use for it at last."

"I like it."

"So, you went to school together?" asked Jack.

"I was at school with his cousin."

"Kate has a barber's shop round on Gibson St."

"Salon," Kate corrected him.

"Do you two want something to eat?"

"I thought you'd never ask."

Rob and Kate sat down in a booth and chatted as Jack prepared some food.

"He's good," said Kate looking again at the pictures on the wall.

"He was ... is a good artist. He did one of our albums covers. He could make something of it, but he's not interested."

Jack appeared with a platter of antipasto.

"This will have to do. Chef isn't in and I'm no cook. Fish and chips, I can do, but not the real stuff."

"Jack's dad ran a fish and chip shop," explained Rob.

"He would have loved this. His son running a proper restaurant. Tuck in."

"So, Jack. Couple of questions for you," said Rob.

"Fire away."

"Scott and Lisa. Do you think they're having an affair?"

"He would like to, that's for sure. If you have it, he wants it. Not sure about Lisa though."

Kate blushed. "I didn't say they were having an affair."

"You're probably right," said Rob.

"Talk to her. Don't guess."

"She's left," said Rob.

"I see."

"The other question was do you mind if I bring someone along to the opening tomorrow?"

"You're welcome to come, Kate."

"No, not Kate. I don't know if you remember Frank McCusker, the writer?"

Jack smiled and shook his head. "Sure," he turned to Kate. "And you are welcome to come too."

\*\*\*

After parking Hugh and Kenny set off on foot back towards Rob's house. Walking along Byres Road they passed by a shop with TVs in the window.

"Shit," said Hugh.

"What?"

"Look, that's her on TV."

"She's gorgeous," said Kenny.

"She's live. That's the lunchtime news."

"You weren't exaggerating. Stunner."

"Kenny, if she's not in, our plan isn't going to work."

"Why not?"

"I only have the number of their house. I don't have her mobile number. The idea was that I get him out of the house and then you phone her."

"Right," Kenny felt relief. "So, is that it then?"

"Let me think. There must be something we can do."

"Let's just go home, Shagger. We can go down the club, have a game of pool, have a drink. This is all madness."

"We need to do it. Come on." Hugh marched into the shop.

"Can I help you?" asked the shop assistant.

"Yes, can you tell me what time the lunchtime news finishes at?"

"Pardon?"

"The lunchtime news. What time does it finish at?"

"Okay. That's a new one."

"You have your TVs on every day, correct?"

"And?"

"You must see this program every day. All I'm asking you is when it finishes. Is that a hard question or something?"

"Shagger, it doesn't matter. Let's go."

Hugh turned and jabbed his finger at Kenny. "Do not call me Shagger. Not here. In fact, don't call me anything."

"Calm down," said Kenny.

"It finishes at two o'clock," said the shop assistant.

"Thank you."

He turned and left the shop with Kenny following on behind.

"What did you go psycho in there for?"

"We don't use each other's names in front of people, Kenny. Now that guy knows something about me."

"Who's going to ask him?"

"I don't know, but that's not the point."

"You said we're not even doing anything illegal."

"It's a little bit illegal, obviously. That's why we need to keep a low profile and not use each other's name in front of people."

"I don't think the police would come up with anything on their computer if they looked for Shagger. It's not your real name."

"Let's just keep it as professional as possible."

"Well, it doesn't matter anyway, if she's not in, does it?"

"It's perfect, Kenny. This works out better. Think about it. If she finishes at two o'clock, she'll be back about half two, three o'clock. I get him out of the house, take him for a drink. You keep an eye out for her. Phone as soon as she arrives back and we're laughing. I think we can do it without using any violence."

Kenny stopped walking.

"Did I miss something? When did we ever discuss violence? What are you talking about?"

"I didn't want to worry you."

"So, what was the plan?"

"The plan was the plan, Kenny. I just had a little contingency, that's all."

"Which was what?"

"If need be, if I couldn't get Rob out of the house, we hold him for an hour or two while Lisa goes to the bank with one of us."

"We actually kidnap him?"

"Only for a couple of hours."

"Shagger, what have you got me into? I don't want to be part of this. I've got a family."

"It was just a backup plan. We don't it need now anyway."

"I want nothing to do with this," said Kenny.

"We're here now. Come on."

"I'm not kidnapping someone, not for two thousand pounds. You said the Brazilians only pretend they've kidnapped someone."

"Well, mostly they pretend."

***

Rob stuffed the packets of crisps into his jacket pockets and carried the drinks over to the table. "Cheese and onion or salt and vinegar?" he asked as he sat down and put the crisps on the table.

"Not for me," said Kate.

"So, do you want to come to the opening?"

"No thanks."

"Really, it's not a problem. You heard Jack."

"What would I be coming as, the rebound chick? No thanks."

"I didn't mean as a date."

"I know, but that's what it would look like. That's what Jack thought I was."

"Did he?"

"Yes"

Just at that moment the song changed on the jukebox. It was Japan singing 'I Second That Emotion'.

"Recognise the song?"

"Did you put that on?" she asked.

"Yeah, doesn't that bring back memories?"

Kate laughed. "Listen Rob, it's been nice reminiscing and all that, but I really don't want to be anyone's rebound date. I work five days a week running a hairdressing salon and people sit down, relax and tell me all the most intimate details of their lives. More than I ever want to know. They tell me all about the breakups and the infidelities and how they are moving on with their lives. And do you know what happens a few weeks later when they come back for their next appointment? They're back together again and the whole thing circles round and round for months at a time. People are never as definite in their opinions about their relationships as they think they are, or as they want to be."

"This isn't a date."

"Good. Do you realise you haven't even asked me if I'm married or seeing someone or have kids?"

"Do you?"

"No."

"It's a good song though isn't it?"

"Yes, it is."

They sat in silence listening to the song. As it ended Kate finished her drink and stood up. "Same again?"

"Yeah."

"What do you think?" asked Rob, after recounting his ideas for Orpheus Jones.

"I think I have absolutely no idea at all. It could be rubbish or it could be great. I just don't know. I think you just have to produce something you'd like yourself and take it from there."

"You're absolutely right. That's exactly what it's like."

"I'm not being profound. I heard someone saying that once in an interview."

Just at that moment a crowd dressed as pirates entered the bar.

"Subcrawl," said Kate, nodding in their direction. "One pub at every subway station. The Doublet seems to be very popular for some reason."

"Let's go for a walk," said Rob.

"I should be getting back to the shop. I have a lot of work to do."

"We can go round the Botanic Gardens and then go for a curry."

Kate paused for a second or two. "Why not, alright. Come on then," she said. "But don't try anything, I'm not interested, okay?"

"If I was taking you on a first date, it wouldn't be for a curry," said Rob. "I tried that once. Didn't work out too well."

***

"Come in," said Fergus Veitch, ushering Scott into his office.

It was not what Scott expected. There were no luxury couches, no trappings of power and status. It looked more like a forgotten storeroom with plastic crates scattered across the floor. The wall was covered in a roll of brown paper littered with post-it notes.

"You wanted to see me?"

"You've surprised me, Scott. The football match on Saturday and then your email. How's the atmosphere out there?" he indicated towards the door.

"Not the best it's ever been."

"I can imagine. It's not an easy job saving a failing company, but that's what I'm doing. Without big cuts this company is going under. It's as simple as that."

"You've been busy." Scott looked around the room.

"I have, and I think I know what's required, but I'm willing to be told I'm wrong. That's why I went to the match with you on Saturday. I know we must drop football, but it's what I was most nervous about. What you said on Saturday, it impressed me. It confirmed what I already knew, but to hear it from you was important."

"So, have you decided?"

"Nothing is ever 100% but yes, pretty much. Have you ever heard of Wu Wei?"

"It's something to do with Taoism isn't it?"

"More than that, Scott. Action through inaction."

Scott nodded as if appreciating what was being said, while wondering where it was all going.

"We cut the expensive program-making and we cut the star salaries. Wu Wei TV. We succeed through inaction, through doing less. This is a local franchise. No one wants to admit it, but that's what it is. There are no real stars, apart from you. Lisa Ward could have an affair with a Vietnamese potbellied pig and it still wouldn't make it into the papers."

"I think she'll make it on national TV," said Scott.

"Sorry, bad example. I know she's your friend's partner. We'll agree to disagree on that one, but you get my point. We need to be smaller, flight of foot. The money we do have to spend needs to be up on the screen. Not spent on expensive rights contracts for sports that no-one watches."

"Where do I fit in? Or is this a farewell conversation?"

"We have obligations. We are obliged by our broadcasting licence to carry a certain amount of local programming. You fit in where you should have fitted in all along. Music. I want you to present a music show."

"What kind of show?"

"Glasgow has a great music scene. We've got every size of venue. We can tap into that. Get bands when they're passing through. Do acoustic sets, maybe getting you playing along with them. But not in a studio. We'd record them at the venues they were playing in. The SECC, Carling Academy, Barrowland. Not during the concert itself though."

"At the sound check you mean?"

"Soundcheck," Fergus paused. "I like it. That's the perfect name for it, Soundcheck."

"I don't know."

"Of course you don't. But think about it and let me know. It could be good for you. It's what you know and maybe it could lead to bigger things. Let me know by the end of the week."

"Okay," said Scott. "It's been a pretty crazy day so far."

"No matter how bad it seems out there, let me tell you, living in the bunker isn't much fun either."

"Is Lisa out of a job?"

"It wouldn't be right to tell anyone else that before she knew, but I thought she had some dog program in the offing anyway?"

"Probably," said Scott. "Nothing's been confirmed yet."

Fergus nodded, "I might be wrong about her, maybe she's a great TV talent in the making."

"You don't rate her?"

"I need to get on. Thanks for coming in to see me."

Scott turned and headed for the door.

"Oh, by the way," said Fergus. "If you do decide to take the gig, it might be a nice opener to do a small acoustic set with the Deltas. I saw you guys play once. You were fantastic."

***

"Maybe they were going out for a meal or something?" said Kenny.

"Maybe," mumbled Hugh.

"We gave it a try, that's the main thing."

"No, the main thing is that we failed. It's cost us over a fiver in petrol, the parking cost six quid, four pounds for tea and for what? Nothing."

"Two pounds for a cup of tea, what's that all about?" said Kenny. "The coffee was even more expensive. It's almost six o'clock. Shona's going to wonder where I am."

"Are you not allowed out after six these days, Kenny?"

The afternoon had not gone well. After getting back to Rob's street, Hugh had left Kenny at the corner and tried ringing the doorbell. There was no answer. They had then stood as far away from the house as they could while still having a line of sight to the front door, waiting for Rob to arrive back. He never did. Neither did Lisa. At five o'clock Kenny had persuaded Hugh to give up for the day. They made their way back to the car, stopping at a café to get a cup of tea.

"What do you think for tomorrow? Should we head in a little later?"

"I'm not coming with you tomorrow, Shagger."

"What do you mean?"

"Just what I say. One minute it's a fake kidnapping, the next it's a real one. I'm out."

"What about Blackpool?"

"Blackpool's good, but it's not that good. I'm not risking going to prison for a weekend in Blackpool."

"So that's it?"

"As far as I'm concerned, yeah."

"One setback and it's all over."

"Yeah."

"I can't do it without you, Kenny. I need someone to make the phone call while I keep Rob occupied."

"If you haven't actually kidnapped him that is."

"Look, I promise not to kidnap him, okay?"

"No, it's not okay. I can't believe I went along with it in the first place. I'm out and nothing you can say will make me change my mind."

"You can have half the money, one thousand pounds."

"I was getting half the money anyway."

"No," said Hugh. "I was paying off Jaffa and then we were splitting the rest. We were getting five hundred each. Look, what we'll do is forget Blackpool. I'll pay off Jaffa and you keep the other thousand. I wasn't really bothered about the weekend away. I just thought that's what you wanted to do."

Kenny shook his head in disbelief. "I was getting five hundred pounds?"

"Yeah, that's what we agreed."

"Five hundred?"

"Yeah," Hugh repeated.

"I was part of a kidnap plan for five hundred pounds?"

"Yes. What's your point?"

***

"Where have you been?" asked Shona as Kenny came into the living room and slumped down in the armchair.

"Popped into Glasgow with Shagger to kidnap his cousin, but he wasn't in."

"Fine."

Kenny laughed. "Is there anything for eating? I'm starving."

"There was, and you weren't here, so I ate it."

"Right. I'll get myself something then."

"Fine."

Kenny stood up and headed back towards the front door.

"Is that you off to the Golden Fry then?"

"Yeah, do want anything?"

Hugh was standing in the chip shop chatting to Armando as Kenny walked in. He bought Kenny a bag of chips and they headed back up the road together.

"What are you going to do about the money you owe Jaffa?"

"Same plan," said Hugh. "I don't have time to come up with anything else now."

"I'm still not coming with you."

"That's alright. It's not your problem."

"I'm sorry."

"I shouldn't suck other people into my problems."

"Fancy a drink?"

"Sure."

# Chapter 6

Rob got to the restaurant early with Frank McCusker. Jack welcomed them at the door but appeared flustered by such early arrivals.

"Don't panic," said Rob. "Just sit us at a table with a couple of drinks and ignore us."

"Okay, but what about Lisa, is she coming?"

"She hasn't been in touch. I'm not sure."

"Haven't you contacted her?"

"I don't know her mobile number."

"You're hopeless, Rob. If she does turn up, do I sit her at your table?"

"I guess so. There's no need to change your plans for us, Jack."

"Remind me of that later."

"Sounds like quite a tempestuous relationship," said Frank.

"Oh, it is. And that was before they split up," said Jack. "Rob, did you see 'Show Us Your Balls' last night?"

"No."

"That moron Rab McBride mentioned the restaurant. He's coming as one of Scott's guests. Made a joke about getting deep fried Mars bars for dessert."

"You should bring one out on platter specially for him. Announce it to the whole restaurant. A special request."

"I don't know."

Frank pulled a pen and notepad out of his jacket pocket and began to scribble away. When he had finished, he ripped the page out and handed it to Jack. He read it slowly and then began to laugh.

"This is perfect."

"You're very well organised," Rob said to Frank after they sat down. "Bringing along a notepad."

"I always have something to ideas down. Don't you?"

"The ideas don't really come that fast. There was a time when they did, but not so much now."

"Until you read Orpheus Jones?"

"Something like that. You know, you can only write so many times about unrequited love, broken relationships and being lovesick before it starts to sound as if it's maybe you that's the problem."

"So, Orpheus solves the problem by being different?"

"I guess so."

"Age-appropriate rock themes for over-thirties. It's a tough nut to crack. I must tell you, Rob, I'm not a big fan of musicals."

"Neither am I. This wouldn't be a musical."

"Good. After I came off the phone to you, I had visions of suicide backpackers doing some kind of Busby Berkeley number surrounded by dancing girls. I don't want to turn up at the premiere to see seventy-two brides for seven brothers."

"Well, at least we're agreed on what it's not. I hate the term concept album, but it does sum up what I was thinking. We would have images or animations from the book thrown up onto the backcloth. We could do it as a one-off performance and see how it goes. If you don't like the result, we shelve it and it never sees the light of day. What do you say?"

"Okay. If I don't like it, you just remove any direct references to the novel. Agreed?"

"I can live with that."

Rob became aware of someone standing next to their table. He looked up to find Lisa staring at him.

"Lisa."

"What have you done to your hair?"

"Oh," he said, running his hands through it. "Just felt like a change. This is Frank McCusker. He wrote Orpheus Jones. He's joining us tonight."

"Nice to meet you again, Lisa."

"Likewise," said Lisa as she noticed the pad and paper on the table. Frank had sketched a caricature of Rob in front of a London Underground sign. "Jesus," she mumbled.

\*\*\*

After talking to her agent, the previous day, Lisa had decided that it might be wise to stay on speaking terms with Rob, at least for the time being. It was over between them, but there was no point it letting it create complications for her. She would go to the opening. Rob wouldn't ruin Jack's big night, so she could be sure of him being on his best behaviour. The other benefit of being on speaking terms with Rob was that it would help finally get the message through to Scott that she wasn't interested in him. He had been practically stalking her since she had stayed the night. Even if she did like Scott in that way, which she didn't, she wouldn't contemplate seeing him now. It was tabloid newspaper material and that was not something she wanted to turn up in the papers while she was waiting to hear about the new show. Lisa had phoned Rob to let him know that she was coming, but he didn't pick up. She left a message on the answering machine.

After arriving at the restaurant Lisa spoke to Jack who pointed her in the direction of Rob's table before continuing to greet the other guests who were now beginning to arrive. As she approached, she thought she had got the wrong table. It was only when Rob looked up that she realised it was him. The short-cropped hair did not suit him. As Rob introduced her to Frank McCusker she glimpsed the sketch and knew that he was serious about the comic musical or whatever it was. He had fallen apart, she decided. He was in the middle of a breakdown.

"I'm sorry for Sunday," she said as she sat down. She squeezed his arm.

"I'm sorry too. I guess we've both been miserable and didn't know how to talk about it."

"Do you two want to be left alone?" asked Frank.

"No, we're fine."

Lisa nodded in agreement.

"Just tell me one thing. Not that it's any of my business, but are you seeing Scott?"

"Absolutely not. What made you think that?"

"It was just something someone said …"

"Did Scott tell you that?"

"Scott? Why would Scott tell me unless you are seeing each other?"

"So, it was him?"

"Right," said Frank, standing up." I'll get some drinks in."

"He wants there to be something and he's willing to lie to make it happen."

"Come on." Rob shook his head.

"He told me you didn't write any songs on the last album."

"That's what that conversation was all about?"

"Yes. He's telling me that you are a liar and he's telling you that he's seeing me."

"Scott didn't say anything to me, Kate just said that …"

"Kate, who is Kate?"

***

Scott was surprised to see Lisa and Rob sitting together when he arrived with Rab McBride. He had expected Lisa to stay away but was glad she was there. He had left telephone messages and looked for her around the TV station but hadn't managed to speak to her since his conversation with Fergus the previous day.

"Hi Scott," said Jack. "Rab, thanks for coming."

"No problem. I was just saying to Scott here, looking forward to the deep-fried Mars bar." Rab laughed at his own repeated joke.

"Well, I'm sure you won't be disappointed."

"Excuse me guys," said Scott. "I'm just going to say hello to Rob."

As Scott approached the table, he could see that Rob and Lisa were quarrelling again. He was about to turn and walk away when Lisa looked up, caught his eye and waved him over.

"Alright, Scott?" said Rob.

"Yeah. I'm glad to see you two back together again."

"Really. Not from what Lisa has been telling me."

Scott froze, unsure what to say.

"I'm sorry, Scott," said Lisa. "What did you expect me to say? You've told all sorts of lies to me."

"I … I," he stumbled for some words. "It's been a crazy couple of days for all of us. All the problems at the TV station."

"What problems?"

Scott sat down and launched into a detailed explanation of the email from Fergus, desperate to steer the conversation away from his own actions.

"Everybody's gone a little crazy, including me. I told him I don't want the job if I have to beg for it."

"Really," said Lisa. "You didn't fight to keep your job?"

"I'm no longer a sports presenter, or at least I won't be once the restructuring has been announced. I spoke to Fergus in person yesterday."

"I'm sorry to hear that," said Rob. "I know it meant a lot to you."

"Thanks. For what it's worth I'm sorry about what I said. I guess when you're under stress you say and do stupid things."

Lisa admired Scott's performance. She didn't think he had it in him. He had declared undying love for her before the email had gone out, but now he'd turned the whole thing around. He had Rob feeling sorry for him.

"He's right," said Lisa. "We've all been waiting for something to happen for months now. That's why I've been so desperate to get the daytime show. I wanted to have something organised before the crunch arrived."

Scott took his turn in admiring Lisa's lies. He wasn't sure what she had told Rob and why she was now backing up his story. He was, however, certain there was self-interest at the heart of it. She was fantastic. She was beautiful and scheming and amoral. She was the woman of his dreams.

Frank McCusker returned with some drinks and placed them on the table.

"I better get back to my guests," said Scott. "But let's talk later."

"Sure, Scott. I guess I owe you an apology, Lisa."

Lisa leaned over and kissed Rob on the check.

"Thank God for that," said Frank as he sat down.

***

Scott winced as Rab spoke yet again about getting a Mars bar for dessert. Their fellow guests at the table smiled politely as Rab laughed at his own joke. The thing about Rab, he had concluded, was that he provided his own canned laughter which helped to convince everyone that he was funny. Outside a TV studio without an audience that had been warmed up, Rab's jokes rarely raised more than a smirk. The main reason people seemed to go along with the illusion that he was amusing was to avoid his attention falling on them. If you laugh with Rab at other people, he would treat you as a member of the audience instead of the butt of the joke. He was tedious company. His humour was based on the humiliation of others.

"Ladies and Gentlemen, can I have your attention," said Jack. "As you know we are a Scottish Italian restaurant and some of you might wonder what exactly that means. Well it doesn't mean we serve haggis with pasta. Burns night was always celebrated in my house though, and we'd like to do our own little version of it here with a special request for Rab McBride."

The door to the kitchen opened and a guitarist came out playing Scotland the Brave, followed by a member of the kitchen staff with a large silver platter and a deep-fried Mars bar sitting proudly on top.

"Ladies and Gentlemen, with apologies to Robert Burns, I give you, To A Mars bar." The guests cheered and clapped as Jack began his address.

*"Hail, chocolate covered fondant bar,*

*Greatest confection near or far,*

*Above them all you take your place,*

*Bounty, Snickers, Milky Way.*


*Wrapper torn, from your body,*

*Dipped in batter, then you're ready,*

*Deep fat fried, until golden,*

*Cut in two, the centre molten.*


*Scotland wants no healthy snacks,*

*Fruit and veg will be sent back,*

*If you want to be held dear,*

*Deep-fried Mars bars raise a cheer."*

Jack picked up a knife and plunged it into the Mars bar.

"For the rest of you, it will be more traditional fare, but Rab, enjoy."

Jack brought over Rab's dessert himself and placed it down in front of him.

"Scott, you were Zabaglione, is that right?"

"Yes, thanks, Jack."

"Wait a minute, Jack," said Rab.

"You did request it, Rab. On more than one occasion if I'm not mistaken."

"Yeah but come on."

"Don't spoil the joke, Rab. It was your joke after all."

"Come on, Rab," said Scott. "We all want to know what it tastes like. Don't we?" he motioned to the rest of the table.

Everyone nodded their agreement.

"What's up, Rab?" said one of the guests. "You on a diet or something?"

Jack motioned over the photographer he had hired for the night. Rab reluctantly took a bite and smiled at the camera.

"You know what? It's not that bad. I couldn't eat a whole one, but a couple of slices with some ice cream on the side. Why not."

"I wouldn't mind a taste," said one of the other guests.

"Me too," said another.

***

"So, it would just be the one show," said Scott.

Rob downed the rest of his beer and leaned back. After the meal had finished, Scott had pulled Rob to one side for a quiet word.

"Even if you're thinking of doing some solo work with this comic guy, you could debut it on the show."

"Soundcheck?" said Rob.

"Yeah, well that was the first name I could think of, but Fergus liked it. It's not signed and sealed yet, but it's looking good. So, what do you say, Rob?"

"Sorry Scott, but I don't want to commit to anything right now."

"Look, you could do a couple of old Delta songs if you don't want to debut new material. I could accompany you. It would be just like old times."

"That's not going to happen, Scott."

"Look, the whole thing with Lisa, it was nothing."

"Scott, it's got nothing to do with what you did or didn't say to Lisa. I am never going to appear on a stage with you again and it's as simple as that."

"Come on, Rob, it's not like you to hold a grudge."

"I don't. When Keith died and we did the tribute concert, that was it finished. You were part of the Deltas. Now that it's gone, it's gone. If I do anything it will be on my own. If you were there on stage, it would be like it was the band to some people and it is never going to be that."

"So that's it?"

"Yeah."

"And what about Jack? Is he to run a restaurant all his life?"

"Yes. He was ready to move on anyway. This is what he's always wanted to do. The last few years, he's not been wondering what to do, he's been planning it. Working for other people, getting to know the trade rather than just rushing into it. This is his dream. Look at the walls, Scott. They're full of his artwork. This place is Jack from the food to the pictures on the walls. He could have done something with his art, he's good enough. He didn't, and the reason he didn't is because this is exactly what he wants to do."

"You could have told me before now."

"I did, you just didn't listen. I told you the night of the last concert."

"We were all drunk, saying all sorts of things," said Scott.

"Yeah, Jack was saying that he was going to open a restaurant and I was saying that the concert was the last ever. Think about it, Scott, I even told the crowd. Of the five thousand people there that night, you were the only one who didn't believe me."

"People say things. They don't mean them."

"Well I did."

"The things I've put off."

"Scott, you've had more of a career than any of us."

"I'm not talking about my career. I'm talking about my life."

Scott threw back his drink.

"What?"

"Lisa. Nothing has happened between us, but it could have."

"You're drunk, Scott. I don't think right now is the time to get into all this."

***

"This is the last one of the night," said Rob. "And it's for Jack. This is about all the conversations you have when you've had too much to drink. It's about saying the good and bad things that you can't normally talk about. It's called 'Drunken Love'."

"If I wasn't drunk,

I couldn't say that I love you.

If you weren't drunk,

You wouldn't hear that I love you,

Funny how it goes,

Funny how it shows,

Saying little things,

Like, I love you."

"Selfish bastard," muttered Scott. "He said he won't perform with me, now he's up there with a pub band."

"Listen, Scott," said Lisa. "I can't be seen with you now. I cannot afford any kind of negative publicity while I'm waiting to hear about the daytime show. Look what happened with Zoe Barton. She's completely out of the running now."

"Who's Zoe?"

"Miss Great Britain, Mrs Jason Barton."

"We are not having an affair, Lisa, nothing happened when you stayed the night."

"Shh! Scott. Do you realise what the papers would make of that? Once it's all died down, we can pick up where we left off."

"What, as friends?"

"Yes. Maybe more, I don't know, but right now we need to be discrete."

"So, you're going back to him, just for show?"

"No, I'm not 'going back' to anybody."

Lisa could feel the situation spinning out of control. Scott was wounded and dangerous. Just after Rob rejected an offer to appear on Scott's new show, he suddenly appeared at the microphone and started singing with the band Jack had hired for the night. To make matters worse it was all Delta songs, Five Thousand Miles, a few old ones and now he was finishing off with Drunken Love. Start the set with a favourite, finish it with a favourite. She had to admit it, he sounded good. The crowd loved it and were singing along, waving mobile phones in the air in the place of lighters. A few were, no doubt, also filming him. Rob's first gig in four years.

The guests roared their approval as Rob finished. He handed back the guitar to one of the band members and shook his hand. He then made his way through the crowd.

"Well done, Rob," slurred Scott. "Hypocritical bastard."

"I'll sing where and when I want."

"As long as no-one else gets the glory"

"I'm not going to argue with you about it. I've told you how I feel. If you don't want to understand it, that's your problem."

"Come on, Scott, there's no point in getting all worked up over it," said Lisa.

"I love you, Lisa, but don't defend him. Not after Sunday. You know what he's like. It's all about him."

"It's not the place for this, Scott," said Lisa.

"Lisa's right. Let's just leave it."

"Is she. And was she right when she called you a talentless shit? When she stayed with me because she couldn't stand to be in the same house as you?"

"Okay, I'm walking away now, Scott."

"The fuck you are!"

Scott lunged at Rob, punching him, before being pulled off by other guests. Lisa shook her head and decided to remove herself from the situation. As she turned, she came face to face with someone holding up their phone, filming the whole thing.

"Fuck."

***

Hugh wasn't sure why he was still there. He had been sitting in the car opposite Rob's house since early evening. He had arrived about six o'clock, only to find the house in darkness. The one good thing was that there were no traffic wardens on duty to chase him away. He had tried to talk Kenny round, more in hope than expectation. Kenny, however, was adamant that he was having nothing further to do with the whole thing, which Hugh could understand. He didn't want to be involved either.

It did make things difficult for Hugh though. As he sat in the car, waiting for Rob to come home from wherever he was, Hugh could think of very few options if doing the job alone. He would have to hold Rob, while Lisa got the ransom. That was assuming they ever turned up. Time had run out for Hugh and it was tonight or never. At eleven o'clock Hugh had been ready to give up and head home. He tried to think of some other source of money but couldn't. At that point he made the decision to sit there all night and all the next day if necessary. There was no other plan.

Just after midnight a taxi pulled up, and Rob got out of the car. He was alone. He paid the driver and made his way towards his house. Hugh got the tights out of his pocket and slipped them over his head. He waited impatiently for the taxi to drive away. The driver appeared to be putting money into a wallet and then stretching under his seat to hide it.

Rob staggered towards the front door, looking the worse for wear. The taxi pulled away as Rob fumbled for his keys. Hugh took a deep breath. If he stepped out the car, there was no going back. He hesitated, watching Rob pull the keys out of his pocket, drop them and then bend over to search for them. Hugh pushed the door and jumped out, his heart beating so hard and fast that it felt as if someone was thumping him repeatedly in the chest. Rob stood up, keys in hand, as Hugh approached him. There was a look of confusion rather than fear as Hugh punched him. Rob fell over moaning as he hit the ground, now dazed as well as drunk. Hugh pulled a pillowcase out from inside his jacket and slipped it over his head. He then turned him round and tied his hands together behind his back with duct tape. Hugh then pulled Rob to his feet and pushed him towards the car, throwing him in the back and slamming the door shut.

He then tracked back and picked up Rob's keys. The street was deserted. Hugh climbed into the car, put his foot down on the accelerator, turned the ignition key and began pumping. The car burst into life. At last, he thought. Something has finally gone right. Hugh took off the handbrake and began the journey back to Pitside.

# Chapter 7

Rob felt groggy and hungover as he woke up. He remembered Scott lunging and punching him, but everything after that was hazy. He tried to open his eyes but couldn't. Screwing his eyes up, he realised there was tape across them. It was then that he remembered the attack. Panic began to set in as he realised, he couldn't move his hands or legs. Another piece of tape was across his mouth preventing him from shouting. Rob moved his legs together trying to kick out at something. The creaking mattress told him he was laid out on a bed. Rob could feel the terror rising in him. He tried, despite the tape, to shout. A muffled groan was all that came out. Breathing deeply through his nose he felt as though he couldn't get enough air and just began to rock wildly from side to side. On his side, he found himself leaning against a wall. He began to kick furiously at it. A door opened to his left and he stopped.

"Stop struggling," a voice said. The voice was low pitched, very slow and artificial sounding. "You will only be here for one day and then you will be released. No harm will come to you. You must not struggle or make a noise."

Rob lay silently, obeying his captor, scared that he would be hit again, the pain now returning to his swollen eye, where he had been hit by both Scott and whoever was talking to him now.

"I'm going now. I will come back if you make any noise."

Rob heard the man leave the room and the sound of footsteps on the stairs.

The memory of the previous night was beginning to come back to him. After Scott had attacked him, Jack and a couple of his staff pulled him off and threw Scott out. Lisa had already disappeared at that point. Rob got back up with the band for an encore as a way of trying to take attention away the situation. It seemed to work, and everyone drifted off happy at the end of the night. Rob sat down with Jack in the empty restaurant and drank a couple of bottles of wine, talking about the band, Keith, Scott and everything in between.

"The strange thing about it all," said Rob. "Is that it was Keith that got Scott into the band, yet Scott wanted to carry on afterwards as if nothing had happened."

"Some people just can't see beyond their own self-interest, and he's one of them. He has no class."

"He has no congruence," Rob slurred.

"Right. Time to call you a taxi, when you start coming out with words like that."

The fresh air hit Rob and he could feel his legs losing their strength. He staggered into the taxi and fell asleep briefly on the way home. It was after he climbed out of the taxi and dropped his keys that he saw the figure moving towards him.

Rob remembered it all now. He also remembered being aware of a belt buckle glinting briefly as he fell backwards. It was a large eagle shape. Rob groaned, realising who had kidnapped him.

He had been kidnapped by Hugh, and was no doubt lying in his bedroom in Pitside. He also realised that he had to do everything possible to avoid showing he knew who his kidnapper was. That could only escalate the situation and it was a risk he couldn't take. Rob wondered if Hugh still lived with his mother, hoping that his aunt was not in on the abduction.

***

"You've got to be joking," said Kenny after shutting the door.

"Keep your voice down."

"You kidnapped him?"

"Well, kind of."

"There's no kind of about it, Shagger. You have kidnapped him. How long would you go to jail for that?"

"It won't come to that. He'll be back home tomorrow."

"I am having nothing to do with this. If that's why you invited me round, then forget about it. This is way over my head."

"I know, keep your hair on. I did it alone and that's fine. I just needed a hand with a couple of things. You just keep quiet and I'll do the talking. Have you got the phone?"

"Yeah," Kenny handed it over.

Hugh opened the bedroom door. Kenny turned to leave. Hugh grabbed him by the arm and pulled him into the room.

"I am going to lift you into a sitting position," said Hugh in his low kidnapper's voice. "Do not struggle. There are two of us."

Hugh climbed onto the bed and lifted Rob by one arm, motioning to Kenny to do the same. Between them, they got him into a sitting position and Hugh stepped over him, back off the bed.

"That will be more comfortable," said Hugh.

Rob struggled, trying to speak.

Hugh picked up a newspaper he had left on the floor and placed it on Rob. He then used the mobile phone to photograph the scene. Rob continued to mumble.

"I will remove the tape from your mouth," said Hugh. "If you make any loud noises you will be hurt. Nod if you understand."

Rob nodded.

Hugh peeled the tape from Rob's mouth.

"I need the toilet. I'm desperate."

"Okay," said Hugh, looking round at Kenny and shrugging.

"And something to drink."

"It's not a hotel."

"I need something to drink," repeated Rob, his voice shaking.

"Water?"

"Anything."

"Okay. We will walk you to the toilet. Do not make any sudden moves."

Hugh put the masking tape back over Rob's mouth and swung his legs round. He motioned Kenny over and the lifted him into a standing position. The newspaper fell to the ground.

"You should be able to make very small steps," said Hugh. He nodded to Kenny and they began to move him slowly out of the bedroom towards the toilet.

Once they reached the toilet, Hugh stopped for a second, trying to work out what to do. He hadn't thought about this side of things and certainly didn't feel like holding someone's penis as they urinated. He turned Rob around.

Kenny held Rob steady as Hugh unbuttoned his trousers. Looking to one side, he then pulled his underpants down and stood up quickly.

"We are now going to sit you down," he said, pushing Rob back.

As soon as Rob sat on the toilet, he let out a groan of relief and emptied his bowels.

"For fuck's sake," said Kenny. "He's doing a crap."

Hugh grimaced at the smell. "We will wait outside. Don't try anything."

Hugh and Kenny raced to get out of the toilet and shut the door.

"I can't believe that."

"He said he was desperate," said Hugh, feeling strangely defensive over his cousin's behaviour.

"I'm sorry, but I just wouldn't do that in someone else's house."

"Well, it's not like he's here by choice, is it?"

"I am not wiping his arse. Don't even ask."

Hugh pushed the door open and looked in.

"Do you think he's finished?" whispered Kenny.

"Are you finished?" Hugh adopted his kidnapper voice. "Nod if you have."

Rob nodded pathetically, slumped on the toilet.

Hugh and Kenny stood him up again and Hugh pulled up his underpants and trousers. Kenny flushed the toilet and they began the slow walk back through to the bedroom.

Rob groaned and tried to speak as they sat him back down on the bed. Hugh partially peeled back the tape again.

"Drink, I need a drink please."

"I will get you a drink."

"This is crazy," said Kenny, after Hugh came back downstairs, empty cup in hand.

"It's just for a day."

"What was the point of the newspaper?"

"Kidnappers always do that, take a photograph with a newspaper. It proves the person is alive."

"How's that?" asked Kenny. "They could just have killed him after they took the photograph."

"Yeah, but it shows that he was alive."

"Obviously, he was alive when he was kidnapped, but you don't need a newspaper to prove that."

"It shows he was alive on a certain date," said Hugh. "The date on the newspaper shows he was alive on that date. So, if you've had him kidnapped three weeks ago and you take a photograph with a newspaper, it shows he was still alive on week three."

"But it would have to be an up-to-date newspaper," said Kenny.

"Yeah."

"That one was from last week."

"You brought last week's newspaper round?"

"You asked me to bring a newspaper, any one you said. It doesn't matter, just any newspaper. That's what you said."

"I meant any newspaper as in it doesn't matter if it's the Sun or the Mirror."

"I don't have today's paper."

"So, when was it from?"

"I think it was Saturday. I usually keep the Saturday paper for the TV guide."

Hugh flicked through the photographs on the phone. He had taken several. The first showed Rob with the paper leaned against him. It was page three with a topless model and the banner 'Brief News'. Hugh had discarded the front page because it had Kenny's name written across the top for delivery. The next photograph concentrated on the top of the paper, large enough to be read if they printed it out. Hugh zoomed in further. Sure enough it was Saturday's edition. He panned down and read Brief News, the topless model's view on some current news story.

'Kerri, 19 from Sutton Coldfield, believes that the fight to establish control of Helmand Province in Afghanistan will involve a battle for hearts and minds that includes respect for the values of the local population.'

\*\*\*

Kate's attention kept drifting as she cut Simone's hair. "I think you should phone him," Simone said to Kate.

"What?"

"You should phone him," she repeated.

Simone was more than a client. She had known Kate for as long as she had the salon and they had become friends over the years. Unlike most clients Kate had, Simone listened to Kate's problems as well as sharing her own.

"It's all very well saying that you should leave it a few weeks, but what's the point if you just spend two weeks thinking about him?"

"I would look like a fool," said Kate.

"And? There are worse things than looking stupid. You've got his number, haven't you?"

"Somewhere."

Kate knew exactly where she had his number. It was written on the back of a parking ticket in the side pocket of her bag.

"Well look it out and give him a call."

"No, I can't," said Kate unconvincingly.

"Just pretend you've lost your mobile phone and ask him if he picked it up. I do that all the time. If he's interested, he'll start a conversation. If not, it's short and sweet and no-one's embarrassed."

"Mmh."

"Just don't phone from your mobile. I did that once. It was messy."

After telling Rob that she wasn't interested in people on the rebound, Kate had gone for a meal with him, ended up back at the pub where they had both got blind drunk and staggered the short distance to her flat. Rob had stayed the night after falling asleep on her couch. They had not stayed up all night talking about the meaning of life and they had not made love. Kate had thrown a duvet over him and staggered off to bed.

The next morning Kate made him a coffee and they both sat on the couch under the duvet not saying very much at all. It was, however, very comfortable not saying anything. There was no awkwardness in their silence.

"I sometimes wonder when I see couples sitting in a pub in silence whether they have nothing left to say to each other, or if they are just happy in each other's company," Rob had said.

"And which is this?" asked Kate.

"You know."

"Well, you can give me a call in a fortnight if you want."

"A fortnight?"

"A seven-year itch is usually cured after a fortnight," she said.

"It's a deal," he said. "But I'll give you my number in case you want to call me."

"I won't."

"That's okay."

"It's stupid," Kate said to Simone. "I don't really know him. We hung around a few times when we were teenagers and that's it."

"I knew I was going to marry Gary the first time I met him."

"The marriage only lasted six months."

"True, but the first three months were good," Simone laughed. "Anyway, does every date need to be Mr Right? Are you not allowed to just enjoy yourself sometimes?"

"I suppose."

"When did you last go on a date?"

"Don't," said Kate.

"Why does this guy have to be perfect before he gets a chance?"

"I know, I know. I'm too serious. I can't help it. That's the way I am. I'm not going to change now."

"Right, well phone him."

"Maybe in a couple of days," said Kate.

"You can't leave it that long if you're going to use the missing mobile phone story. You're pushing it already."

"Okay, okay, I'll do it later."

"Kate, take a two-minute break and go and phone him right now."

"I'll do it at lunchtime."

"Do it now. I can wait."

"All right."

She left Simone, went into the back office and got the number from her handbag. Kate took a deep breath and dialled the number quickly before she could change her mind. The phone rang three times and then went on to the answering service.

"Hi," she said, after the tone. "It's me. I lost my mobile and wondered if you picked it up by accident. Give me a call if you have it. If you've still got my business card that is. If not, you could just pop in and let me know. Well, pop in if you have it, or if you're just passing. Don't worry though if you can't make it. If I don't hear from you, I'll just assume you don't have it. I'm rambling. Sorry, I hate leaving messages. Oh, did I say who it was? It's Kate. It's me, Kate."

"Well, how did you get on?" asked Simone.

"I have just made a complete fool of myself, but apart from that, fine."

"What did he say?"

"Nothing. I have just rambled on incoherently to his answering machine like a star struck fan."

"Give him a day and then phone him back if you don't hear from him."

"You must be joking?"

"No, I do it all the time. Just tell him you found your mobile and you thought you'd let him know in case he's just got the original message."

"Have you ever thought that you're maybe going about it the wrong way, Simone? Maybe I should be giving you advice instead of taking it. Are you happy?"

"I might not be happy, but I'm having a good time."

\*\*\*

Kenny flicked on Colin's computer and played with the mobile phone while he waited for it to start up. He knew what he was looking for. He needed to make a Bluetooth connection to the computer in order to download and print off the photographs. He had watched Colin do it many times before but never really paid much attention. Colin pretty much spent his life on the computer when he wasn't at school. Kenny found it hard to see the attraction, but it seemed to keep Colin out of trouble.

The computer had been one of fifty gifted to the people of Pitside by a Government initiative called the Digital Exclusion Task Force. Although it sounded like a combat unit, it was two ex-social workers in a rented bus which doubled up a classroom. Kenny had not been keen on taking one, but Colin had begged him, so eventually he agreed if it was installed in Colin's room. The computer came with a two-year broadband connection, free of charge.

The thing that had made Kenny suspicious of taking one was the fact that they were tagged. The PCs had software installed that reported back on usage on a regular basis to the Task Force. Kenny had been convinced that everything done on the computer was visible to some government department. Quite why they would be interested in what Kenny was doing on the computer, he had never figured out, but the whole thing seemed very suspicious. The real reason for the monitoring was a lot less complicated. The first wave of computers had been given to every house in a community just outside Dumbarton. As soon as the computers had been delivered, most of them were sold on, much to the embarrassment of the Task Force. The monitoring software simply confirmed that the PCs were still connecting to the internet from the original broadband connection.

Kenny couldn't find the Bluetooth connection on the phone. He could get back into the photographs but couldn't work out how to send them to the computer. He looked around the desktop of the PC to see if anything obvious jumped out at him. It didn't. He was defeated and just about to switch the computer off when Colin came in through the door.

"Mum said you might need a hand."

"You back for lunch then?"

"I come home from school every day for lunch."

"I was just trying to print off some photographs from your phone. I can't get the Bluetooth to work."

"You haven't plugged in the Bluetooth USB adapter. How's it going to work if you don't do that? It's not a laptop. It doesn't come with Bluetooth as standard."

Kenny's eyes glazed over.

"Do you want me to do it?"

"Would you, son? That's great. It's these two photographs here." Colin flicked back and forward between the two pictures of Rob and the newspaper.

"What's that meant to be?" asked Colin.

"Just a practical joke, that's all. Could you print both photos on the one bit of paper?"

"Okay. What is this practical joke anyway?"

"Nothing. Just something Shagger's doing. Don't mention it to anyone though. Don't want to spoil it."

***

"There's no need to apologize," said Jack. "It was all over in a flash anyway. I don't think many people even noticed."

"But it was your big night," said Lisa. "I didn't want to take anything away from it."

"I don't think you did. Even if you did, it would be more publicity for the restaurant anyway."

"Publicity is the last thing I need right now. I'm up for a daytime show and one whiff of bad publicity and it's over."

"Rob mentioned."

"Did he really? He's been so dismissive of my career. That's what's killed our relationship."

"Well, that's between the two of you."

"There is nothing happening between me and Scott, I swear it."

"Like I said, none of my business."

"Scott has been interested, but he never got any encouragement from me. I just tried to stay friends without leading him on."

"Really. I don't want to know."

"I just don't want you to think badly of me. You've been a good friend to Rob, despite everything, and I've always admired you for that."

"Despite what? Rob's always been a good friend to me too."

"But he broke up the band, didn't he? Killed off the career."

Jack sighed. He didn't want to get sucked into Lisa's conversation and had been trying to get rid of her, but he couldn't let this one pass.

"That's Scott talking," he said. "When Keith died, we all agreed the band was finished. If I'd wanted to stay in music I would have."

"Why did neither of you do it then?"

"Because we were no good. What are the chances of four friends being equally talented in the same field? If you're lucky two of them might be, and the other two make up the numbers. We were lucky. We had Keith and Rob. Me, I wasn't a particularly good drummer. I was a friend of a couple of talented guys and I got to go along for the ride. When it came to an end, I went off and found out what I was good at, and this is it."

"What about Scott?" asked Lisa.

"Same deal. But he loves the fame. So instead of finding something he's good at, he found something that would keep him famous."

"Scott said that Keith wrote all the songs on the last album. Rob had lost it."

Jack shook his head. "I don't think so."

"He said that Keith could write songs in the style of anyone and that he wrote Rob's songs."

"Keith wrote Keith's songs and Rob wrote Rob's songs. For the record though, it is Rob who is the mimic. He's got a whole collection of fake Beatles songs. Some of them are better than the songs we released."

"I don't really know him," Lisa mumbled out loud.

"Look, I don't mean to rush you, but I need to get on now. The lunchtime crowd will be turning up soon."

Lisa stood up. "Okay, thanks for listening."

Jack walked her to the door of the restaurant. "When you find what you're good at, it's the best feeling in the world. Much better than any accidental success. You stop waking up with that feeling that you're about to be found out. It's worth the search."

"I know. I had the same feeling the day after I presented my first lunchtime show." She kissed Jack on the cheeks and walked towards her car.

Hopefully he will relay the conversation to Rob, she thought, as she got into the driver's seat. I don't want Rob as an enemy. I'll give him a phone later once Jack has had a chance to talk to him.

*\*\**

Hugh let himself into Rob's house and quickly closed the door behind him. He reckoned he was too early for Lisa to have arrived back yet, but he stood silently for a second or two listening for any noise. He couldn't hear a thing but decided not to take any chances and pulled the tights over his head. He looked at himself in a mirror. He shook his head. Hugh reckoned it was still pretty obvious who he was. Perhaps he should have chosen a thicker pair. Still, Lisa had only met him once, so maybe it was okay.

Hugh's plan was to wait for Lisa to appear. He would then hand over the pictures of Rob and make his demand in person. He had originally planned to confront them both the previous night. When Rob had turned up alone, he had improvised. They obviously led quite erratic lives, but he would wait if it took all night for Lisa to appear. He would then get the money off her and let Rob go. Time was getting tight, but he reckoned he could get the money before Jaffa came looking for it.

Hugh made his way round the ground floor of the house. Entering the kitchen, he stood in awe at the refrigerator. It had two doors which opened from the centre to reveal a well-stocked interior. One shelf was stacked with beers, mostly Budweiser. Not the American version but the Czech one in the large bottles. Hugh had tried this version before but wasn't too keen on it. It had quite a strong flavour. The tasteless American version was better for consuming large amounts. Hugh took one of them out and placed it in the freezer section. He reckoned he could afford to have one drink while he waited, and if he could cool it to the point just before it began to freeze that would kill the flavour. He then browsed through various cupboards until he found one with snacks. Hugh laid a selection out on the work surface and decided to go with the Macadamia nuts, not having tried them. He ripped open the packet and pulled the tights up above his mouth.

Hugh continued his tour eating the nuts and marvelling at how well Rob had done for himself. Two thousand pounds wouldn't even dent his bank account. Entering the cinema room, he let out a sigh of appreciation. Wall-mounted flat screen TV. At least fifty inches, but Hugh reckoned more like sixty, high def and, looking around the room, there was a surround sound system in place as well. The killer, however, was the chairs. Four full-leather Lazy Boy recliners. Hugh sat down and pushed back. This, he thought, this is living. Hugh finished off the nuts sitting on the recliner just staring at the TV. He didn't need to switch it on. It was enough to be sitting on the chair, eating nuts and staring at it.

After finishing the macadamias, Hugh pulled the tights back down over his mouth. As he did so a ladder appeared over his nose. This was no good. He would be recognised now. Hugh made his way upstairs and found Rob and Lisa's bedroom. Hugh tried several drawers until he found some underwear. He shook his head in admiration. The drawer was a treasure chest of beautiful garments,

Every colour imaginable was there. Hugh took a handful out and threw them on the bed. He held a pair up and marvelled at them. They were blue silk with side ribbons that tied together in a bow. Shaking his head and trying to concentrate, he opened the next drawer. This one had only tights. Again, he pulled a selection of tights out and threw them on the bed. Examining one pair he realised it was a pair of hold ups, tied together. Unravelling them he noticed that the seam was the shape of a snake. Hugh took the old tights off his head and pulled on one of the snake hold-ups. He looked at himself in the mirror. The snake appeared to be making its way up his neck. He put the spare leg in his pocket and picked up the rest of the tights to put back in the drawer. As he did so, he noticed a DVD case. Hugh dropped the tights on the floor and picked up the disc. There was no writing on it, but the position of it in a drawer, full of lingerie, excited Hugh's imagination. He headed straight back downstairs to view it in the cinema room.

***

Lisa looked down at the newspaper page again. The column was entitled 'Glasvegas', and it was the gossip column in the free evening paper. There was a grainy picture of Scott attacking Rob. The headline was 'West Coast Belters'. The story did not mention Lisa by name, but it was implied.

*The launch party for the new restaurant of former West Coast Delta drummer, Jack Baldini, ended in a bust up between his former bandmates, Rob and football pundit Scott Kilbride. One witness described how Delta's front man Rob had just completed a surprise set to celebrate the opening of Fratello Scozia when Kildride lunged at him in a violent and seemingly unprovoked attack and 'belted him in the face'. Although it was not clear what the cause of the fight was, one insider explained that there were rumours of a love rivalry between the former bandmates. Rob's partner is a TV colleague of Kibride's. Whatever the reason, it is unlikely that there will be a reunion of the band anytime soon.*

"This could lose me my job," said Lisa stabbing at the article.

"They don't mention you," said Scott.

"Has anyone from the papers been in touch?"

"No, it's one paragraph in a gossip column."

"What are you going to say if anyone does get in touch?"

"Nothing."

"Nothing. I don't think so. You can say that it was nothing to do with any love rivalry. You were just drunk and upset that Rob played without you."

"Why would I say that?"

"Because it's true and because if you don't and my name ends up the paper, I'll tell them you've been stalking me and spreading lies about Rob to try and break us up."

"Are you back with him?"

"No, but that's not the point. You will not destroy my career. Do you understand?"

"It's a free paper. It's not a real gossip column. People read it on the bus on the way home from work and then bin it. This isn't going to make it into the nationals. It's not that important, Lisa"

"Well thanks for that opinion, but if you could excuse me, I need to speak to my agent."

"Phone me later."

Lisa was still smarting from Scott's assessment of their celebrity status as she explained the situation to her agent. She did not want to tell him but knew that he would know what to do.

"I don't think it matters," he said. "Don't worry about it."

"But what about the Zoe Barton thing?"

"Well, that's different."

Lisa should have been pleased but she wasn't. "How is it different? It wasn't Zoe that did anything wrong, but you said it doesn't matter in daytime TV."

"I know, but it is different. She's a wag, the gossip columns love wives and girlfriends of footballers. Especially if they're models or beauty queens."

"But they love TV personalities as well."

"I know," he said. "You will be big, Lisa, but right now you're not. You're a regional star. You're not big enough just yet to be worth knocking down. Build them up and knock them down. That's how it works. You're still being built up so you're okay for the time being."

"So, I'm less interesting than the girlfriend of a footballer?"

"Not to me," her agent said. "Don't offended by it, it's just the way it is, and it works in your favour. Unless you have a sex tape that's about to hit the internet, you have nothing to worry about."

"Why would you say that?"

"You don't, do you?"

Lisa's face reddened unseen by her agent as she made her excuses and got off the phone.

\*\*\*

The phone rang in the hall just as Hugh passed it. He jumped, as if caught out, and then stood silently waiting for it to stop. After a few rings it went to the answering machine. Hugh listened as Lisa left a message.

"Hi Rob. It's Lisa here. Hope you're okay after last night. I've had a word with Scott and told him that he was out of order. I think he must be having a mid-life crisis. Anyway, I hope we can stay friends. I'll pop round tomorrow after work to see you and we can talk everything through. Love you."

Hugh couldn't believe it. They had obviously broken up. That was why she wasn't with him the previous night. He decided to play the message again in case he had misunderstood. If they had split up there was no one to give the ransom demand to. The only other person was Rob's dad and that just wasn't something he was willing to do to his own uncle. Hugh fumbled around with the answering machine and eventually managed to get the messages to play. As the messages played Hugh recognised a voice but couldn't quite place it. Then she left her name. It was Kate. His Kate. She was phoning Rob and chatting away as if they were the best of friends.

When did this happen? Was Rob seeing Kate behind Lisa's back? Is that why they split up? What a bastard! What a lucky bastard.

Realising that Lisa would not be coming home that night, Hugh took the stocking off his head and fetched the beer from the freezer. It was perfect. Ice cold. Hugh looked out another packet of nuts, cashews this time, and headed through to the cinema room.

"Hi Kenny, it's Hugh here."

"Shagger. Where are you? I thought we were going down the club when you got back?"

"I'm still at Rob's house. There's been a development."

"You've not done anything to his girlfriend?"

"No, they've split up. She's not here."

"Are you drunk?"

"Just a little, too much to drive though, so I was wondering if you could pop round and give Rob a drink of water for me?"

"Are you joking?"

"No, I don't want him to dehydrate if I'm leaving him overnight. You're the only one with a key."

"When are you coming back?"

"Tomorrow, first thing."

"Okay, but that's all I'm doing. I'm not taking him to the toilet."

"Fine. I'll see you tomorrow."

Hugh hung up the phone and fetched another beer from the freezer. He was well gone now but he didn't care. He staggered back to the cinema room and un-paused the DVD. He still couldn't quite believe it. Rob and Lisa having sex. It wasn't like most of the celebrity sex videos, shot in the dark with poor lighting. This was perfectly clear in all details. Lisa did a strip tease routine and then they got down to it. The camera was either resting on a piece of furniture or occasionally picked up for close-ups. Once or twice when the camera was resting on furniture, Lisa and Rob moved position to be certain that they were in the shot. Hugh couldn't believe it. Hugh had searched the bedroom for other DVDs, emptying every drawer in his search, but this was it. The one and only. Not that it mattered. Kenny's boy could make copies for him. His troubles were over. He didn't know who he could sell it to, but he knew a man that did. Jaffa would know what to do with it. This would more than clear his debt. Jaffa was the source of 'Glasgow Amateurs' DVDs in the village, and claimed that he knew Pierce Mahone, the guy that directed most of them. Hugh reckoned that he could even make some money himself. Jaffa would know how to sell the story to the papers and then distribute it. They could make thousands. All he had to do now was let Rob go, which he would do the following day, and everything would be good.

\*\*\*

Rob had lost track of time lying in the dark. It seemed like days since he'd last been visited. He knew it wasn't, but it seemed that way. Hugh had clearly left the house as the place was in complete silence. Rob had wet himself after holding on for as long as possible. After that he had cried. It wasn't fear, or at least it didn't feel like it. He just felt helpless and wetting himself had been the thing that tipped him over the edge. The tears loosened off the adhesive on the masking tape and although he couldn't see, he could open his eyes partially and tell whether it was light or not. When darkness came, he cried again, then gave himself into trouble for doing so. He decided he must think about something, anything, to keep the despair away. Despair was his enemy and he must fight it at all costs. Rob forced himself to think back over the Orpheus Jones Story, his new project.

Orpheus, once he discovered the underworld below the Tube, contacted a group calling itself The Deceased Organisation of Agnostics. The D.O.A. helped Orpheus search for Izzi amongst the members of the various death cults. As Orpheus travelled with them, they explained how death had not solved any arguments. Various groups believed their current existence was a waiting room for something better. The hardcore atheists believed they did not really exist, and the suicide bombers felt that they hadn't killed enough people to go straight to heaven.

After much searching, Orpheus found Izzi and begged her to return to the overworld. Izzi agreed, but on ascending, she began to cry uncontrollably. She explained that she was no longer of this place and could feel nothing. She could not smell the world or taste or feel the world. The light was too strong for her and she saw everything as if through a veil. Orpheus took her back to the underworld and told her he would stay. Izzi told Orpheus to go back to the overworld and live while he was living, to embrace the world through his senses, just as she had to embrace the underworld. 'We'll always have Hackney', she said, referring to Orpheus's love of the film Casablanca. They parted company and Orpheus returned to the surface.

Rob began to truly understand the attraction the story had for him for the first time. His grief had lasted a long time and the reality was that he had not got past it. He had not felt that he should get past it. That would be somehow dismissive of the dead, disrespectful. As a result, he had ended up living inside his grief. It was not what his mother or Keith would have wanted. It was a half-life. He had found himself these last few days feeling truly alive again. Sitting under a duvet talking to Kate, singing in front of a crowd at the restaurant, seeing Jack creating something new and celebrating it, without ever forgetting. Fratello Scozia was Jack's, but it was also something that his father would have appreciated. He was remembering the dead through life instead of through grief. What had Rob done? Anaesthetised himself with drink and avoided his father as much as possible. Orpheus Jones would be his way of living without forgetting, his Requiem, where the living remembered the dead. Rob decided that he would get out of this. He had to. No matter how helpless he felt, how humiliated he was, he would accept it. He would get through it to the other side and when he did, he would spend his time working, spend time with his father, he would spend time sitting in the company of people he liked, sitting in a cold flat under a duvet, drinking a cup of coffee, saying nothing at all. All this was what he decided he had to believe in, what he had to focus on. For the first time since being taken, Rob felt, not exactly peace of mind, but a sense of acceptance that he must do whatever it took. The only thing that he still had to resolve in his mind was where that moron of a cousin had been for so long.

***

Kenny approached Hugh's house slowly. He knew that the more he helped him out, the harder it would be to avoid sharing the consequences if Hugh was caught. Kenny imagined being found in Hugh's house during a police raid. He wanted nothing to do with any of it.

Shagger was good fun to be around, he thought to himself, but lately he'd lost the plot. Trying to kill himself and then kidnapping his cousin. Kenny decided that as soon as he'd given Rob some water that was it. He wasn't going to see Hugh for a while. He would spend more time with Colin, maybe even learn a bit about the computer. He would go for walks with Shona during the day. Clean his act up. No more hanging around the club, day in day out.

"Alright, Kenny!"

Kenny looked up startled. It was Jaffa standing at Hugh's door.

"Any idea where Shagger is?"

"Eh, no. I was just looking for him myself. Is he not in?"

"No, and his door is locked. That's kind of unusual, isn't it?"

"Is it?" said Kenny.

"Yes, it is," said Jaffa, moving towards Kenny and lowering his voice. "The door's usually open, and if it's not, the key is under that plant pot. Kind of looks like he's gone away somewhere. You wouldn't know anything about that would you?"

"Not me. I saw him today. I was just coming to see if he wanted to go down the club. Maybe he's there already."

"He's not," said Jaffa. "Funny thing is, he owes me some money. I wouldn't like to think that he's avoiding me. That would be kind of irritating."

"I'm sure he'll be back tomorrow."

"What a strange thing to say."

"I don't know where he is, Jaffa, I'm just saying he'll probably be back tomorrow."

"There you go getting all specific again. Saying tomorrow. Not saying soon, or some time, but saying tomorrow."

"I don't know why I said that, Jaffa."

"Probably because you are kind of nervous and because you know a little more than you're letting on."

"I don't. I mean he could be at his cousins or something, but I don't know."

"You're doing that specific thing again."

"Honestly, Jaffa, I don't know where he is."

"You and Shagger are pretty good friends, best friends even. So, here's how it goes. If he doesn't turn up and pay me the money he owes, you are going to inherit his debt."

"I haven't got a thousand pounds."

"You see? You even know how much the debt is. That's how close you two are. He tells you everything, like where he's going. And here's the thing. That makes you partly responsible for him. Anyway, I can't stand around all night chatting. Need to be off. If you see Shagger, let him know that I'm looking for him and I'll pop back over tomorrow."

"Okay."

"Oh, and if I don't see him. I will see you."

Kenny watched as Jaffa got into his car and drove off. He looked around the street. No one seemed to be around, but he couldn't risk it. He decided Rob would just have to wait and headed down to the club for a drink. Why couldn't Shagger even kill himself properly?

***

Kate read the article about Rob's bust up with Scott and felt glad that she had not gone to the opening. Perhaps Lisa and Rob had made up and that was why Scott had attacked him? How many people really split up the first time they split up? Kate did. Her first break up, with Hugh, had set the pattern. If you are going to break up with someone once you will do it again, so why drag it out? If you're breaking up, just do it and get the pain over and done with. Yet all the evidence of friends and customers told her that she was just the only person that acted so decisively.

Perhaps that's why he hadn't returned her call. He was back with Lisa and didn't want to compromise things. Nothing had happened yet something had. If Kate could freeze time it would have been sitting with Rob in her living room, both slightly hungover. It was nothing and it was everything. Working as a hairdresser Kate made physical contact with people all the time. That physical contact was what made people so willing to share their most intimate details with a stranger. Yet it was false because it was not reciprocated. The customer relaxed, but she worked. Sitting next to Rob, their arms touching. Two people touching, just touching and being in each other's company.

Kate decided that she could not torture herself like this anymore. If Rob was back with Lisa she had to know and put this fantasy behind her. She looked out his number and dialled. The answering machine kicked in again. Kate sighed.

"Hi, this is Kate again. It's just to say that I found the mobile ..." Kate heard a click at the other end. "Is that you Rob? Have you picked up?"

"Uh, no. He's not here," said a drunken slurred voice. "I'll pass the message on for you."

Kate recognised the voice immediately. "Hugh?"

"No!"

"Hugh, I would recognise your voice anywhere. Where is Rob?"

"Eh, well. He's not in, but I'll pass on the message. Are you two going out with each other or something?"

Kate paused. "Fuck off, Hugh. It's got nothing to do with you."

"I know, I'm just asking."

"Where is he?"

"I've got to go. I'll maybe see you the next time you're up at Kenny's though, eh?"

"Thanks for the warning," Kate said as Hugh put the phone down on her.

# Chapter 8

Hugh woke up at lunchtime on the Lazy Boy chair. It was comfortable, but not comfortable enough to get a good night's sleep on. Hugh's neck ached from the position he had adopted as he fell into a drunken stupor the night before. After watching the home-made porn video several times over, Hugh looked through the DVD collection for something else to watch. He had come across *Apocalypse Now*. It was fantastic with surround sound. He felt as if he was in the movie during the helicopter scene. The fact that he had managed to drink every bottle of Budweiser only added to the experience. After losing control of his limbs and sitting back on the recliner Hugh was practically having an out-of-body experience. He had switched the lights off and the room was bathed only in the glow of the TV screen. He felt like a spirit-being, floating around the action rather than a viewer watching it.

Now, as he woke up, he did not feel like a spirit. He felt like a lump of rock. His body was heavy, and it was an effort even to keep his head up. Hugh shuffled through the kitchen and made some tea and toast. He took a bite of the toast and then realised that he was in no fit state to eat. He spat the toast out onto the plate and held his tea with both hands. He would need a few hours to recover before he could make his way to the car for the drive back to Pitside. After arriving at Rob's house, the previous day, Hugh drove slowly through the area looking for a street without controlled parking. He was at least a mile from Rob's house. He could have got closer by using a car park, but funds were beginning to run low and the last thing he needed was the car being clamped.

Despite his sorry state, Hugh felt content for the first time in weeks. He was certain that the DVD of Rob and Lisa would resolve all his problems. Taking his tea, he shuffled through the hall, not sure where he was going. The phone rang. Hugh ignored it and carried on walking, vaguely recalling talking to Kate the previous night. He shook his head. Surely, he'd imagined it after hearing her voice on the answering machine. He'd probably just listened to her message again.

"Are you still there, Shagger?" came a voice from the phone. "Pick the phone up."

Hugh stared at the phone in disbelief.

"Shagger, pick up the phone," Kenny shouted again.

Hugh lifted the receiver. "How did you get this number?"

"You phoned me last night, remember. I just did 1471."

"What is it?"

"When are you coming home?"

"I'm not sure, Mum. What time's dinner at?"

"Jaffa was looking for you last night."

"He didn't find Rob, did he?"

"No, but he was at your door. I couldn't go in."

"You mean you haven't seen Rob? He could be in a bad way. For Christ's sake, Kenny. You were responsible for him."

"Jaffa's coming back tonight. He told me. He's looking for you and if he doesn't find you, he'll be looking for me instead." Kenny recounted the conversation in full.

"It's meant to be Friday before I pay him. Why's he looking for us already?"

"How many tickets have you sold for Friday night? That's why, and don't start with all that 'us' business."

"Don't worry, Kenny. I have got everything sorted. Trust me. All we need to do is let Rob go and everything is fine."

"I hope you're right."

"Kenny, we will make a lot more than two thousand pounds, trust me. Jaffa will be more than happy with what I've got to give him."

***

Kenny entered Hugh's house quickly after looking left and right. He shut the door behind him. Hearing moaning and banging as soon as he shut the door he went straight up to the bedroom. The smell of urine hit him as he opened the door. The crumpled figure on the bed continued to moan and kick the wall.

"I'll take the tape off if you promise not to shout," Kenny said.

The figure nodded pathetically. Kenny bent over the bed and peeled back the tape from Rob's mouth.

"I need something to drink," he croaked. "And something to eat, please."

"I don't think there's much for eating, and I can't stay that long anyway."

"Anything, please. A piece of bread."

"I'll see what I can do," said Kenny. As he tried to put the tape back on, Rob turned his head away from him.

"Leave it off please. I won't make any noise."

"Okay," said Kenny.

There wasn't much to give him. He made a jam sandwich and poured a glass of milk. Heading back up the stairs Kenny thought about how polite Rob was. Please this and thank you that. It reminded him of his gran. She always insisted on please and thank you. Colin never said either to Kenny, but then again, he didn't insist on it. Things aren't the way they were, he thought as entered the bedroom. He put the glass and plate down and lifted Rob up into a sitting position.

"Sandwich coming," he said as he put the bread up to Rob's mouth.

Rob took a bite and chewed furiously.

"Sorry about all this."

"More please."

"I'm not really part of all this," he said feeding Rob another bite. "In fact, I tried to talk him out of it. He'd already done it before I could stop him. I'm not a kidnapper. I just agreed to look after you while he went into Glasgow. If I hadn't agreed you would have been left here alone. That doesn't make me a kidnapper."

"No," said Rob. "A drink please."

"He's always coming up with some scheme or other, but this is the worst."

"Another drink please."

"I spoke to him this morning though and I told him. This ends today. You let him go or I'm contacting the police. He's finally seen sense. Once he comes back, he'll pick you up and drop you back off in Glasgow. Don't cause any trouble with him and it will all be over soon. I promise you."

"Thank you. Another drink please."

"I'll be honest with you. Once I've got you out of this, I'm having nothing more to do with him. I told him on the phone. I said, Shagger, we're finished."

Rob's head slumped.

"I mean it."

"Another drink please," said Rob, but much quieter this time.

"I need to go now. I'm sorry, but he'll be back soon."

"My trousers."

"Sorry, but I can't stay any longer."

Kenny put the tape back over Rob's mouth. "He shouldn't be too long."

Kenny looked around as he left the house. There was no one in sight. He ran the short distance to the end of the road and began to walk, breathing deeply. Shagger should release him later, he thought, but if anything goes wrong at least I have told him I had nothing to do with it. A sudden embarrassing realisation crept into his thoughts. He had said 'Shagger' to Rob when he was talking to him. He had told Rob who the kidnapper was.

As Rob heard the front door close, he thought, I must escape. There is no other way now.

***

Lisa had bought a copy of every tabloid newspaper, local and national and checked through them. Not one had anything about the fight at the restaurant. She knew she should have been pleased, but a small niggling voice in the back of mind told her that this was a bad thing. Why was no one interested in her? She wasn't seeing Scott, but it would be very easy to suggest that she was if the papers wanted to. Was she really that uninteresting? Okay she was still mainly known in Scotland, but there had been France *avec* Ward.

Even if the papers had not considered her interesting enough, what about Rob and Scott? They had filled stadiums. Was the story of two bandmates fighting over the same rising TV star not worthy of at least a couple of column inches? Lisa decided that she had to face facts. Rob was no longer that famous. He'd left it too long and now he was forgotten. People still recognised him, but as far as the media was concerned, he was no longer of interest. Scott had tried staying in the limelight, but despite his enthusiasm for the new music show, it was a step backwards. It would be aired just before the overnight phone-in quiz started. He was one step away from being a late-night DJ. Scott didn't even realise that he was sinking.

Lisa just had to wait and pray that Doghouse Makeover happened. In the meantime, she would go back to Rob's place and get the DVD. She was certain that Rob wouldn't do anything with it, but there was no point in leaving it to chance. She would have a chat with him about staying friends and then get some clothes and the DVD.

There was only the one copy. Lisa knew because it was her that had transferred it to the disc. They had made it early in the relationship. They were just fooling around with the camera treating it like the new toy that it was. Before they knew it, they were in the bedroom starring in their very own movie. There was something incredibly sexy about the idea of it. The reality was a little different as the positions and angles they had to maintain to get any decent footage tended to take away from the spontaneity of the whole thing. She had both enjoyed watching it, but Lisa had always intended to destroy it at some point.

*** 

Scott wasn't sure he wanted Lisa anymore. The bust-up in the restaurant had got a lot of things out of his system. He'd always wanted to punch Rob. Even when they were in the band together, he would like to have punched him. If fact, Scott reckoned that he would probably never tire of punching Rob. He always acted as if he was the leader, Keith was second in command, and Scott and Jack were just hangers on. Making up the numbers. Okay, Keith and Rob wrote all the songs, but a band is a band. Fair enough Jack was not a particularly good drummer, but Scott liked to think he brought something to the party. The trouble was that Rob never acknowledged it. Never let him do any solos, never let him really develop his persona beyond that of a glorified backing musician.

The strange thing was, now that he had hit Rob, he realised that once was enough. As he had been dragged off Rob by other guests, he was secretly relieved. He didn't have the heart to carry on. Scott reckoned that Rob would be nursing a shiner of a black eye and that felt good, but that was it. He had made his own way in the world, and now he was getting his own identity within the music business as a host. How long does any star last these days, he thought? Three years if you're lucky, but hosts go on and on.

And then there was Lisa. Suddenly no longer that attractive to him. Was it because she wasn't with Rob? Did he only want her because she was with him? Maybe a little, but it had been more than that. When he joined the station as a sports presenter, Lisa seemed like the seasoned professional. Everything he wanted to be, successful, confident, in control. It was all an illusion. Fergus had helped him see that.

"Tell me, Scott," he'd said as they passed in the corridor that morning. "Anyone take pictures of your big bust up the other night?"

"Sorry about that, Fergus," he said. "We were all just drunk. It won't happen again."

"You're a musician, Scott. That's what musicians do. You're meant to behave badly. But did anyone take any pictures?"

"A few folks on their mobile phones I think."

"And how many of them made it into the paper? None. All you managed is a few columns in a free newspaper."

Scott was confused. "Are you disappointed, Fergus?"

Fergus laughed. "No, just wondering if you still think Lisa's such a big star, that's all."

Scott replayed the comment over and over and contrasted it with Lisa instructing him to deny everything if approached by the papers. No one had approached him. She was not a star. She was a TV presenter. That was the start and end of it. She was a TV presenter who was no longer going out with someone who was no longer famous. Scott laughed at what a fool he'd been. It was Scott that was going somewhere not Lisa. Football had been a false start to his new career, but at least it was a first step on the ladder. He had made all his mistakes there and could now start on the real thing. He'd found his direction in life. What's more the late-night slot would give him the freedom to develop the show in a way that a prime-time slot wouldn't. There would be less restrictions. He knew that because Fergus had told him.

\*\*\*

The fresh air was helping Hugh to sober up as he walked back to the car. After taking the call from Kenny, Hugh had deleted all the messages from the answering machine in order to scrub Kenny's voice. He then went back upstairs and had a shower in the en-suite bathroom in Rob's bedroom. The hot water of the shower felt good and he sat down to let it fall on him like rain. After what seemed like an hour he got back out of the shower, padded back downstairs in the nude and made himself another tea. Hugh felt good walking around naked. For a reason he could not quite comprehend, it made him feel as though the house was his. There was no logic to it, but that was how he felt.

Hugh had then taken his tea back upstairs and lay down on top of their bed. Lisa's tights and underwear were still spread around, and he liked the feeling of them. He shut his eyes for what he intended to be a second or two and woke up a few hours later. Looking at the time he quickly got dressed, gathered up the DVD and some snacks, mostly nuts and crisps, and a couple of bottles of spirits. The spirits were single malt whiskies which Hugh didn't really like, but he could dilute them with ginger ale or maybe even swap them down the club for some vodka.

Walking back to the car, Hugh imagined himself living in Rob's house. This was him just out for a walk. Strolling past large sandstone villas. This was the life that he should have. This was a life that would make him happy. Hugh smiled and said hello to people as they passed. Not many of them returned the greeting. Most looked down and walked slightly faster until they were past him. This puzzled Hugh. Here they all were, living the good life, yet they didn't even smile at each other in the street. At least for all its faults, nobody ever walked past you in Pitside without acknowledging your presence.

Hugh was now getting the hang of the car and it started first time. Heading off back towards home, he thought about how best to release Rob. Another trip back into Glasgow didn't appeal to him. He was tired and just wanted to have a couple of pints down the club and then get an early night. Hugh decided that he could probably let him go in Hamilton. Rob knew Hamilton, so if Hugh dropped him off there, he would be able to find his bearings quickly. He could get the late bus home or even just spend the night with his dad.

Hugh drove along Woodlands Road heading towards the motorway entrance, but the traffic was heavy, and it came to a stop every ten feet or so. Gazing out the window as the car was stationary Hugh suddenly caught sight of Kate. She saw him and walked towards him. He stared straight ahead at the car in front and hoped she hadn't seen him. Kate banged on the side window of the car. Hugh glanced quickly to the side and looked straight ahead.

"What were you doing at Rob's?" she shouted.

Hugh continued to ignore her, urging the traffic to start moving again.

"Where is he?" she shouted.

The traffic started up again and Hugh drove off without making eye contact. Christ, he thought. I did talk to her last night. Suddenly, things were not looking so good anymore.

Kate phoned her sister from her mobile phone as she watched Hugh drive off. Something was going on. She didn't know what, but something wasn't right. Kate's nephew Colin answered the phone.

"She's down at the chip shop. Will I get her to phone you back?"

"Yes, thanks Colin. Listen is your dad still hanging out with Hugh?"

"Shagger? Yes."

"What are they up to these days?"

Colin paused too long. "Nothing."

"Right. Well maybe if you could get your mum to phone me."

"Do you know something?"

"What is there to know, Colin?"

There was another silent pause. "I don't think Mum knows anything."

"Right, what about you, Colin, what do you know?"

"I don't want to get him into trouble."

"You're not going to get him into trouble but tell me what you know."

"I think they've maybe kidnapped someone. Dad said the picture was a practical joke, but it didn't look like it to me."

Kate paused this time before speaking. "What picture, Colin?"

"They used my phone to take it."

"Is the picture still on your phone?"

"Yes. He told me to delete it, but I didn't."

"Can you send it to me? You've got my number on your mobile, don't you?"

"I don't know. What about Dad?"

"I'll sort this out, Colin. Don't worry but send me the photograph right now."

Kate began to walk towards her car. Her phone rang once. Kate flipped it open and pressed read. The photo took a few seconds to load. When it did, she recognised Rob immediately.

***

Lisa opened the door and popped her head in, shouting as cheerfully as she could manage.

"Rob, it's me, Lisa."

There was no reply. Lisa went into the kitchen. It was a bit of a mess. Half the food from the cupboards was out on the work surfaces. There was a plate of toast with one bite taken out of it and then spat back onto the plate. Rob was a bit of a slob, but he'd never been this bad. Lisa shouted again. Still, there was no reply. She walked through to the cinema room and stopped in her tracks at the door. Beer bottles lay strewn around the floor with empty packets of nuts and crisps taking up the gaps.

Lisa was now getting worried. Making her way up the stairs she slowed as she approached the bedroom, worried that she might find him in a broken-down state or worse. What she saw disturbed her more. The entire contents of her lingerie chest had been emptied out over the bed. Lisa shouted for Rob again at the top of her voice. There was no reply. She searched frantically though the underwear for the DVD, then looked in the empty drawers. It was gone and so was he. Lisa sat down on the bed, picked up a cushion, held it to her face and screamed at the top of her lungs.

"No, I've not seen him," said Scott, his voice sounding disinterested over the phone.

"I've tried everyone else I can think of," said Lisa. "His dad, Jack, that comic book writer. No one's heard from him since the night of the fight."

"Well, he's hardly likely to get in touch with me."

"You're not being very helpful."

"He's nothing to me, Lisa. Yeah, I was jealous of him in the past, but that's in the past. I'm moving on."

"But I'm worried about him. What about me?"

"What about you?"

"What's wrong with you?"

"Like I said, I'm moving on. I'm starting over. You've made it clear that there's nothing between us. I can handle that, Lisa. There's nothing between us."

"But we're still friends."

"If you want to be, sure. Listen I need to go now. I'm meeting some people for a drink tonight. Phone me tomorrow if he's not turned up. Speak to you later."

Lisa sat on the bed, stunned. Still holding the phone, not quite able to believe that Scott had hung up on her.

Must keep going, she thought. Keep going.

Lisa put the phone down and slowly stood up. Where are my GHDs, she thought as she looked for her hair straighteners.

\*\*\*

Rob turned his arms as a far as he could in opposite directions loosening the masking tape. Because his hands were behind his back it involved a great deal of effort, even for small movements. After a few minutes, he had to stop due to the cramp that developed. He waited for it to subside and then started over again. After an hour, he was finally able to free his hands by sliding out of the now stretched loop of tape.

When he freed his hands, he cursed himself. Why hadn't he tried before? Because he never knew how much time he had before Hugh would come back. He started on the tape securing his arms above his elbows. He moved his shoulders up and down, again in opposite directions loosening the tape. With his wrists no longer secured, he managed to reach up with one hand and tug the tape down and free his arms. Pulling them in front of himself he hugged himself and massaged his limbs trying to get the circulation back.

He then pulled the tape from his eyes and mouth. The light hurt, so he shut his eyes again while he removed the rest of the tape from his legs and ankles. Rob knew he might not have much time. He stood up and then fell back down on the bed. He hadn't been aware of it, but his legs were numb. He slapped them and tried again. This time he stayed up, but he knew he didn't have much energy to draw on. Rob made his way down the stairs slowly, holding on to the banister and listening for any noise as he went. As he reached the bottom, he thought he saw a figure through the frosted glass of the front door. Still not sure of the strength in his legs he turned and made small, rapid, steps through to the kitchen. The back door was locked. He looked around desperately. A key was sitting on the work surface. He tried it in the lock, and it turned. Rob stepped outside into the garden and looked around to get his bearings. The house backed onto fields. He continued with his baby steps as he marched through the garden, climbed over the low fence and made his way across the field.

It was dusk and the light was beginning to fail. If he could just get a decent distance away and hide for a few hours in the dark, he would be fine. Rob tried to remember the place from his visits years before, but it all seemed different to him. Then he spotted some lights flicker on in the distance. He made his way towards it, thinking that it must be near a road. Rob ached all over and his thighs were beginning to sting as they chaffed against the urine-soaked trousers. He kept going. This was to live, he told himself. Keep going. After a few hundred yards, he could make out his destination in more detail. A figure dressed in blue and white was illuminated, hands outstretched as if welcoming him. From this distance, it looked a little like the Blue Nun that appeared on the wine bottle, but Rob recognised it from his last visit to Pitside, it was the grotto of Mary's Junction. The place he'd sat and talked about his future with Kate while Hugh lay semi-conscious next to them. That was where he was heading for. It was his goal. If he could reach the grotto, he would be fine.

***

Hugh drove into Pitside in a depressed state of mind. Just when everything had been looking good, he had ruined it. As soon as Rob spoke to Kate, which they clearly did on a regular basis he would know who had kidnapped him. The thought fleetingly occurred to him that he could kill Rob and hide the body, but he knew he couldn't do it. Hugh didn't think of himself as being a bad or evil person, just someone who found himself in an awkward situation. Killing Rob would cross the line. He was still pretending to himself that he hadn't kidnapped Rob. He'd just borrowed him for a couple of days. He was no longer looking for a ransom, he hadn't even demanded a ransom, so technically he hadn't kidnapped him.

Hugh decided to tough it out and just release Rob anyway. He would deny everything. Kenny could give him an alibi.

As he drove up to his house, Hugh saw Kenny approaching the door. Kenny turned, saw Hugh and waited for him. He did not look happy. Hugh was later than he intended, but it was not as if they could do anything with Rob till it was dark anyway. He jumped out of the car and attempted to appear upbeat.

"Kenny, cheer up, everything's under control."

"Maybe not."

"You worry too much."

"I mentioned your name in front of him."

"What?"

"I was feeding him and just chatting, and you know, I just kind of said Shagger without thinking."

"You've got to be kidding?"

Kenny shook his head. "What are we going to do?"

"I don't know," Hugh, brushed past him and opened the door.

"I think you should just own up and let him go."

"Thanks for that advice, Kenny. When I own up, will I mention you?"

"I had nothing to do with the kidnap, Shagger."

"Thought so." Hugh headed up the stairs.

As he pushed open the bedroom door, he sensed something wasn't right. The silence was too complete. The door swung open to reveal an empty bed and fragments of tape scattered across the floor.

"He's gone," said Kenny.

Hugh's mind reeled at the shock of it. "Thanks for stating the fucking obvious."

Kenny walked over to the bed, as if to check that they weren't just imagining it. He looked out the bedroom window and squinted.

"Is that him?"

Hugh pressed his face against the glass. "He's heading for the grotto."

Hugh turned and ran down the stairs and out of the house. If he took the road, he could catch up with him.

Running down the street, he passed the shop. Davy was putting some rubbish out. He noticed Hugh and shouted over.

"Shagger, have you got a minute?"

"Not right now, Davy. I'm in kind of a rush."

"My cousin got a last-minute cancellation for tomorrow night."

Hugh stopped for a second. "The Karaoke?"

"Yeah, the Karaoke. Do you still want him? He's got most of the fee from the cancellation, so he'll give you a good discount."

Hugh looked into the distance for no more than a second but thought at a thousand miles an hour. Why did he care about Karaoke when his life was falling apart? But then again, Davy's cousin always put on a good night. But it was too late to drum up interest. But if it was a discount price maybe it didn't matter. But he'd probably be in a police cell tomorrow night. But a Karaoke night took care of itself.

"Okay. Seven thirty start?"

"No problem, I'll let him know."

Hugh continued his pursuit. As he approached the grotto he had to stop and get his breath back. He wasn't used to such vigorous activity. He looked around, searching for Rob. Hugh swore, thinking that he had lost him. He leaned against the drystone wall and looked at the figure of the Virgin Mary. There was a foot sticking out from behind the structure. Hugh climbed over the wall and leaned forward, resting his hands on his legs as he tried to get his breath back.

"I know you're there, Rob."

Rob stood up and stepped out from behind the Virgin Mary. "So, what are you going to do about it? Kidnap me again?"

***

Jaffa was driving towards Pitside as he saw Hugh cross the road at the grotto. This was ideal. He was coming to see him anyway and had intended to take him somewhere quiet and private. The grotto was a perfect spot. Hugh had not seen Jaffa as he climbed over the wall. He braked and turned into the car park.

Jaffa had popped into the club the previous night and discovered that they had only managed to sell twenty tickets. If Hugh was going to pay Jaffa back, it was not from ticket sales. The fact that Hugh seemed to be avoiding him tended to suggest that he had not raised the money. That meant, unfortunately, that he had to be punished. Jaffa got out of the car and collected his gun from the boot of the car. It was a sawn-off shotgun. Not the best weapon in the world, but perfect for intimidation and individual acts of punishment.

Jaffa entered the grotto to find Hugh with someone else. Someone he did not recognise.

"Shit. That's all I need."

Jaffa let one round off into the air. Hugh spun round wide-eyed at the noise.

"Both of you, get over beside the virgin where I can see you."

"Jaffa, everything's okay. Let me explain."

"Move now," he shouted.

Rob and Hugh stood side by side, illuminated by the light coming from the grotto.

"Christ," said Jaffa, noticing the similarity for the first time. "There's two of them. Who's this, a long-lost brother?"

"He's my cousin. Listen I'm okay for the money."

"Well that's a surprise. It's good though. Hand it over then."

"I don't have the money, but I have something better."

Jaffa snorted. "So, you don't have the money?"

"Like I said …"

"So, you don't have the money?" Jaffa shouted.

"No but let me explain."

Jaffa sighed. "Okay, both of you, undo your trousers and drop them."

"That's it," said Rob. "I've had enough. Shoot me if you want, but anything else, fuck off."

Jaffa laughed. "Relax, it's just to stop you making a run for it. It's kind of hard to run with your trousers round your ankles. Wouldn't you agree? Now drop them."

"Listen Jaffa," said Hugh.

"Drop them, now."

Rob undid his belt and unzipped his trousers, aware of Hugh doing the same. He pushed the wet trousers down over his thighs and straightened up, no longer caring what happened next.

Jaffa stared at Hugh's crotch. "What the fuck is your game?"

***

Kate arrived in Pitside to see Kenny running along the street towards her sister's house. She slammed on the brakes.

"Where is he?" she shouted at him.

Kenny came to a dead stop. "Who?" he said unconvincingly.

"Rob, Is he at Hugh's house? You better tell me right now or I swear I'm calling the police."

Kenny just wanted to crawl away and hide somewhere. He had completely lost the will to lie. "They were both going in the direction of the headless virgin."

Kate turned the car and drove off towards the grotto.

The scene that met her when she reached it disorientated Kate completely. Jaffa was standing with a shotgun pointed at Rob and Hugh. They were standing in front of the grotto, backlit, with the Virgin Mary staring out from behind them. Their trousers were at their ankles and Hugh appeared to be wearing a pair of blue silk embroidered underpants with white side ribbons tied in a bow.

"Oh, join the party, why don't you?" said Jaffa. "Over there beside them." He pointed with the barrel of the gun.

"Are you okay, Rob?" asked Kate.

"I don't really know."

"Why have you got women's underwear on Hugh?" she asked.

"We were all wondering about that," said Jaffa. "Please, enlighten us."

"I think they're Lisa's," said Rob.

"And are we expecting this Lisa to join us as well?" asked Jaffa.

"He was in your house last night," said Kate. "I phoned and he answered. He said you were away."

"Okay," said Jaffa. "You two, shut the fuck up. Shagger, what is this all about?"

Hugh's shoulders slumped. "I just liked the feel of them against my skin. It's like you're pressing against a woman. I'm not gay or anything."

"I'm not talking about the fucking knickers. I'm talking about all of it."

"I tried to borrow the money I owed you off Rob, but he refused. So, I kidnapped him. But when I went to deliver the ransom, he'd split up from his girlfriend and there was no-one to give the ransom demand to. While I was in Rob's house, I was looking through his girlfriend's underwear and I found …"

"I don't want the whole fucking story of why you chose those particular pants, thanks all the same."

"No," said Hugh. "I found a …"

"Let me get this straight," said Jaffa. "You kidnapped someone over one thousand pounds?"

Rob looked round at Hugh. "A thousand pounds?"

"That's what I was asking you for at the funeral. It's not as if you can't afford it."

"You kidnapped me, left me lying in my own piss for two days, for a thousand pounds?"

"You haven't seen what he does to people that owe him money," said Hugh.

"Hugh, you never even checked my wallet the whole time you had me. I've got a couple of hundred in cash and I've got a bank card."

"Oh."

Jaffa shook his head. "Why him?"

"He's Rob, the lead singer of the West Coast Deltas," said Hugh.

"Five thousand miles?" said Jaffa. "That band? The phone adverts?"

"Yeah, he's loaded."

Jaffa shook his head again. "Shagger, you really are a moron, aren't you? Just supposing you had managed to deliver the ransom note. Let's think this one through. First, is anyone going to take a one-thousand-pound ransom seriously?"

"I was going to ask for two thousand," he answered defensively.

"Oh well, that makes all the difference. Another little thought though. Did you think the police wouldn't be involved when a celebrity had been kidnapped? How did you think this would end?"

Hugh shrugged.

"Rob, may I call you Rob?"

"If you let me pull my trousers up."

"Sure. You just stay as you are though, Shagger. Rob, why didn't you give him the money?"

"He didn't tell me the full story, but even if he had, I wouldn't have believed him, or given it to him."

"Okay," said Jaffa, nodding. "When people owe me money, I do tend to inflict a little damage on them, it's true. Shagger here, is going to give me a thousand pounds or I'm going to blow a hole in his kneecap. He'll recover but will walk with a limp. On the plus side, he will be in no fit state to ever kidnap you again. Question is, knowing the full facts as you now do, are you willing to lend him the money?"

Rob looked at Jaffa and realised that, not only was he serious, but also that Rob would witness the punishment if he refused. Despite everything he'd been through he had no stomach to watch another person being tortured.

"Okay."

"Right," said Jaffa. "Here's how it goes. You give me your wallet and pin number for your bank card. I'll return it when I've got the money out. Don't worry, I will only take a thousand. I am a man of my word. What's the daily limit on your card?"

"I don't know," said Rob.

"We'll sort it out. Don't worry. One other thing though. We are going to have to make sure that you don't go to the police."

"He won't," said Kate. "Honestly, it's all forgotten."

"I'm sure that's all true, but I think we need to make sure. I'm thinking that if you appear in public it would be kind of hard to claim you'd been brought here under duress."

"Good idea," said Hugh. "Does anyone fancy a drink down the club?"

"Pull your trousers up and shut your mouth," said Jaffa. "We have a little club night here tomorrow. If you appeared at that and sang a few songs that would be great. Folk out here don't often get to see quality acts."

"I don't know," said Rob.

"I do know?" said Jaffa. "It's not a request. I'm just making it sound like one."

"Right, well okay then."

Jaffa lowered the gun, walked towards Rob and held his hand out for the wallet. "It's a deal. It will mean a lot to the people here. I'll see you tomorrow night then. I'm thinking you could do a couple Sinatra numbers. I know that's maybe not your thing, but hey, it works for Rod Stewart, it could work for you."

"Okay then," said Rob. "See you tomorrow Jaffa?"

"Call me Bill. I'll never get the folk round here to call me anything else, but the name's Bill, Bill McVitie."

"Can I just clear one thing up?" said Hugh. "If you're getting the money off Rob, does that mean that the club gets to keep any money from tomorrow night?"

"I suppose so," said Jaffa.

"It's just that it will help with the ticket sales."

"Shagger?"

"Yeah?"

"Shut the fuck up before I change my mind."

\*\*\*

Lisa sat in the dark contemplating her future. Maybe Rob wouldn't do anything with the tape. Whatever else he was, drunk, insensitive, unappreciative and moody, he hadn't ever been vindictive. But then again, why would he take it with him.

Lisa's phone rang. She grabbed at it.

"Rob?"

"It's Brian. Bad news I'm afraid."

Lisa's heart sunk. "Tell me."

"There's no easy way to say this. Doghouse Makeover isn't going ahead."

"Who got it?"

"No one. I mean the show isn't going ahead. They've pulled it."

"Why?"

"It's like a franchise, Lisa. Once one program appears on a theme the franchise is taken. Some other independent has been pitching a show about a dog psychologist. Apparently, she's a cross between Barbara Woodhouse and Supernanny. Anyway, they've decided to go with that for the next season. Doghouse Makeover may still happen at some point, but not for the moment."

"So, what do we do now?"

"We keep looking for a good vehicle for your talent. Don't lose heart. The big break is coming. It's like a train, it might be delayed, but it will turn up."

"I know."

"I'll be honest, you're taking it better than I thought you would."

Any news that didn't involve Lisa turning into a reluctant porn star was no more than a small disappointment. "It's just a program, Brian. Like you say, others will come along. Listen I've been thinking. I'm not sure I'm cut out for daytime TV. The whole moral side of it is all a bit hypocritical, isn't it? Is there anything a bit more cutting edge in the pipeline?"

"Well, there is another show. 'Sex after Marriage'. A therapist helps divorcees rediscover their sexuality, that kind of thing. They're looking for a presenter, but I didn't think that was your thing."

"Let's go for it."

"Cool!"

***

Hugh stood alone at the grotto. He didn't think it was a good idea to ask Kate or Jaffa for a lift back up to Pitside, besides which he felt like being on his own. He stood looking at the Virgin Mary, her hands stretched out to embrace all who approached. He had never really looked closely at her before. He had thrown stones at her and attempted to decapitate her but never studied the statue. She was beautiful, but not in a sexy way, just beautiful. She had a kind face and a forgiving smile. She had to be forgiving, living so close to Pitside, with all the hate that had been thrown her way over the years.

Hugh decided that she was the perfect mother. She was the mother a four-year-old sees. The mother that knows everything you have done and will forgive you anyway. The mother that only has your interests at heart and loves you regardless. She wasn't the mother an adult has. The mother who joins singles clubs and heads up north with the aging village lothario. That was okay though. His mother deserved a life that didn't involve being perfect, because she had been perfect when he was four. She was perfect when it mattered.

The Virgin Mary let those Catholics have a perfect mother even when they were adults. Even when they didn't have a mother. Nothing an adult could do would surprise her, was beyond her forgiveness.

Christ thought Hugh. Those Catholics have it easy. Everything forgiven.

"Mary," he whispered. "Could you forgive me?"

The statue continued to stretch her hands out in welcome, continued to smile, continued to say nothing.

"That's good enough for me," said Hugh.

## Chapter 9

Gordon had not been looking forward to doing the second Back to Work session in Pitside. They weren't the worst group of people he'd ever had, but the place was so bleak and depressing that he found it hard to maintain the act of motivational role model. His lack of enthusiasm was quickly overcome. Hugh, who had shown some small signs of progress the previous week, came marching into the class like a man who had discovered himself.

"Can I just say something before we start?" he asked.

"Sure."

"I've been organising a night at the social club. It's on tonight, and the tickets haven't been selling that well to be honest. So, I used that as the focus of my homework. Six degrees of separation. Who do I know that could help me turn the night around? That's the question I asked myself."

"That's good," said Gordon. "Using a real-life situation. How did you get on with it?"

"It was hard, but I've finally started getting the hang of it. I thought to myself, what do I need to add to the night."

"That's all very well," said one of the other attendees. "But no matter what you do it's still a fundraiser for the U.U.F. A lot of people don't like that."

"What's the U.U.F?" asked Gordon.

"It's a terrorist organisation," said Hugh. "But that's not important, they've been dropped."

"A terrorist organisation?" said Gordon, eyes wide open.

"Dropped?" said someone else.

"Yeah. I told Jaffa that it was putting people off, so he agreed to withdraw. Tonight, is now a fundraiser for the club. I was thinking we could raise money for a large flat-screen TV and maybe even a surround sound system."

"That would be great for the football," said John.

"Or even movie nights," said Hugh.

There was a murmur of approval.

"Anyway. Davy's cousin has a mobile Karaoke business, and I've booked that. All at a discounted rate. Armando is donating a couple of free fish suppers as a raffle prize. We've got a few crates of beer as another prize, and my cousin is going to come along and sing."

"That one that was in a band?" asked John.

"Yeah. Rob from the West Coast Deltas"

"You're joking," said Gordon. "He's your cousin?"

"Yeah. He's coming. I'm hoping he'll do a Karaoke duet as a raffle prize as well. Sing one of his own songs. The winner can get their photo taken with him, signed autograph, the whole shooting match."

"I'm speechless," said Gordon. "In all my years of doing this, I've never had such a positive reaction. Really, this is amazing."

"It was the balloons that did it," said Hugh, winking over at Sarah. "But the thing is. This all just came together last night. No one knows. So, I thought to myself this morning. Who do I know that can help publicise it? Six degrees of separation and all that. Then it came to me. All of you here. I don't want to take over your course, Gordon, but how about we knock up a few posters and leaflets and spend the day getting them around the village? There's a computer in the office here. If you paid the janitor for the paper, he'd let you use it. What do you say?"

"We'll put it to a vote," said Gordon.

"Free entry for all of you," said Hugh. "And your first drink is free. No cocktails though."

***

Lisa was called into Fergus's office as soon as she arrived at the TV station.

"You're dropping me from the lunchtime show, aren't you?"

"I am. We're cutting costs where we can, and I don't think people tune into the lunchtime news for entertainment. To be honest not many people watch the lunchtime news at all. It's a franchise obligation so we can't drop it completely, but there's no point in adding bells and whistles to it."

"Okay. I do have a three-month notice period."

"I know, and we will honour it."

"You've got to."

Fergus smiled. "I know."

"So, do I finish in three months or do I sit at home and collect my salary?"

"I haven't worked out the exact timescales yet, Lisa, but I believe in getting all the bad news out the way as quickly as possible. You're not going to go postal on air though, are you?"

"Postal?"

"Crazy"

"No, I do intend to have a career after this."

"Yes, you're up for some dog thing, aren't you?"

"Doghouse Makeover. It's been delayed though."

"Oh, sorry to hear that. Anything else on the horizon?"

"There's a few other possibilities, but nothing definite."

"You know I've offered Scott a program?"

"Soundcheck?"

"Yes. He's not the best presenter in the world, but I think he's got a name that will help. People in the music business remember each other long after they've stopped working."

"I suppose."

"Anyway, it could do with a real presenter to hold it together. Keep Scott on track. He's still got a way to go. I need a mentor to work with him."

"Is that an offer?" asked Lisa, surprised.

"I used to work in consultancy, you know. One of the biggest mistakes I saw small and medium size companies make was that they would get too dependent on one customer. Spread the risk. Get more small contracts, that's what I always told them. You're a small company, Lisa. Everyone in this business is. Let me be honest with you. You're not a star, but you are a professional and competent presenter. Soundcheck wouldn't be a big contract, but it would give you some work and leave you space to do other things as and when they came along. You would be the main presenter. Scott's job is to attract the talent."

Lisa smiled. "Have you discussed this with him?"

"Not yet."

"Okay."

"Take time to think about it."

"I've thought about it. Okay."

\*\*\*

Rob entered the club with Kate as the Karaoke was being set up. He'd spent the previous night at her sister's house. Kenny had been thrown out and told to spend the night with Hugh. Kate's sister apologized for her husband's part in the kidnap and Rob reassured their son, Colin, that his father was not going to prison. He then soaked in a hot bath and went to bed. He didn't sleep too well. He kept waking up imagining that he was still at Hugh's house, still trussed up and unable to move. Kate lay beside him on the bed, holding his hand whenever he woke up.

The next morning, he chatted to Colin over breakfast about comic books. Colin was not a fan of McCusker and the Orpheus Jones book, but had read it. He preferred Neil Gaiman and the later Sandman stories. Rob then went back to bed with a pile of Colin's comics and had an afternoon sleep.

Rob and Kate went to the club early to get the music organised. The guy setting up noticed them entering the hall and came over to introduce himself.

"Hi, I'm Daljeet. Davinder's cousin. I run Singh Sing Karaoke."

"Right," said Rob.

"You the guy that's going to sing the Sinatra stuff?"

"Yeah."

"I'll get the book and you just let me know which ones you want to do."

"Right."

"Apparently, you're going to do '5000 miles' with a raffle winner to finish off?"

"Am I?" said Rob, assuming this was another 'request' from Jaffa. "Fair enough."

***

Rob didn't mind Frank Sinatra, in fact he had a few CDs in the house. It's just that he'd never considered singing the songs in concert before. Rod Stewart didn't use a karaoke machine that displayed the words on a screen for the crowd to sing along to. This crowd did sing along. 'The Tender Trap', 'My Way' and 'New York, New York' to round the set off. For the last song they crowd formed a circle holding hands and danced in and out, as if singing Auld Lang Syne.

"Okay," said Daljeet. "We're going to finish off in a minute, but can I just have Hugh up to announce the grand total for the night."

Hugh took the microphone. "Thanks for the support you've shown tonight. We've raised over one and a half thousand pounds tonight. The most we've ever managed."

"Well done, Shagger," someone shouted.

"While I've got all your attention, could I ask you all to stop calling me Shagger. I'd like to be known as Hugh from now on."

"Ooooh," the crowd said collectively, followed by a chant of "Shagg – er, Shagg – er."

Hugh shook his head. "I'd also like to thank my cousin Rob who's going to sing a last song with me. It's one of his own, so join in if you know it."

"Did you win the raffle then?" Rob asked.

"No, but they're all bastards and don't deserve it." Hugh nodded to Daljeet.

A marching beat that sounded nothing like '5000 miles' started, and the first line of the lyrics appeared on the screen.

*When I wake, well I know I'm gonna be*

"That's '500 Miles' by The Proclaimers," Rob shouted over to Daljeet.

"I know, but it's better for singalongs than yours," he shouted back. "Everybody knows it."

"When I wake up, well I know I'm gonna be," sang Hugh.

Rob, noticing Jaffa singing along at the front of the crowd, decided he better join in.

***

Rob and Kate were walking back from the club when Hugh caught up with them.

"I just wanted to say thanks again, Rob."

"You know what, Hugh? I didn't want to see you get shot, but I don't forgive you."

"I know." Hugh looked and sounded quite upbeat. "I don't expect you to. I really don't."

"Right. Well, that's good to know."

"Maybe once you've had time to get over all this, we could meet up for a drink sometime?"

"I'm thinking that's kind of unlikely."

"Like I said, once you've got over it. You know, Rob, I learned a lot about myself this week."

"Well, I'm glad it's been an opportunity for personal development."

"It has. I've been too down on myself. Lacking in confidence. I think this week has been a turning point for me, it's a junction. I know now that I can do and achieve things if I really put my mind to it."

"Well, that's great."

"I left your house in a bit of a mess. I didn't damage anything. I just mean that I didn't tidy up before I left."

"Any other confessions?"

"I took this," he handed over an envelope.

Rob opened it and looked inside. It contained the remains of a DVD which had been cut up into small pieces.

"I was going to do something with it, but it just didn't seem right."

"Lisa and me?"

"Yes, sorry."

"Well, I think that's the first decent thing you've done."

"Like I said, I've passed a junction. Changed direction."

"Right, well I'll see you at the next family funeral then, Hugh."

Kate and Rob got into the car and she started the engine. Hugh bent down and tapped on the window.

"What?" asked Rob after lowering his window.

"I've kept Lisa's knickers. I didn't think she would want them after I'd had them."

"I think you're right. Goodbye."

Hugh waved as they drove off into the night.

"What did he give you?" asked Kate.

"An indiscretion. I can go into details if you really want."

"No thanks."

"So, look. I know you've got this two-week rule and everything, but do you fancy going out sometime?"

"Okay," said Kate. "I'll break the rule just this once. Do you want to come back to my place? I didn't have any plans for tonight anyway."

"Me neither."

The End

Printed in Great Britain
by Amazon